"There.
You're all
set."

"Thanks,
oniichan."

AMANE HANA

RIN'S SIXTEEN-YEAR-OLD SISTER. SHE'S
ABOUT TO MAKE HER ADVENTURER
DEBUT, BUT SHE POSSESSES A SECRET
TALENT...

THE WORLD'S FASTEST
LEVEL UP

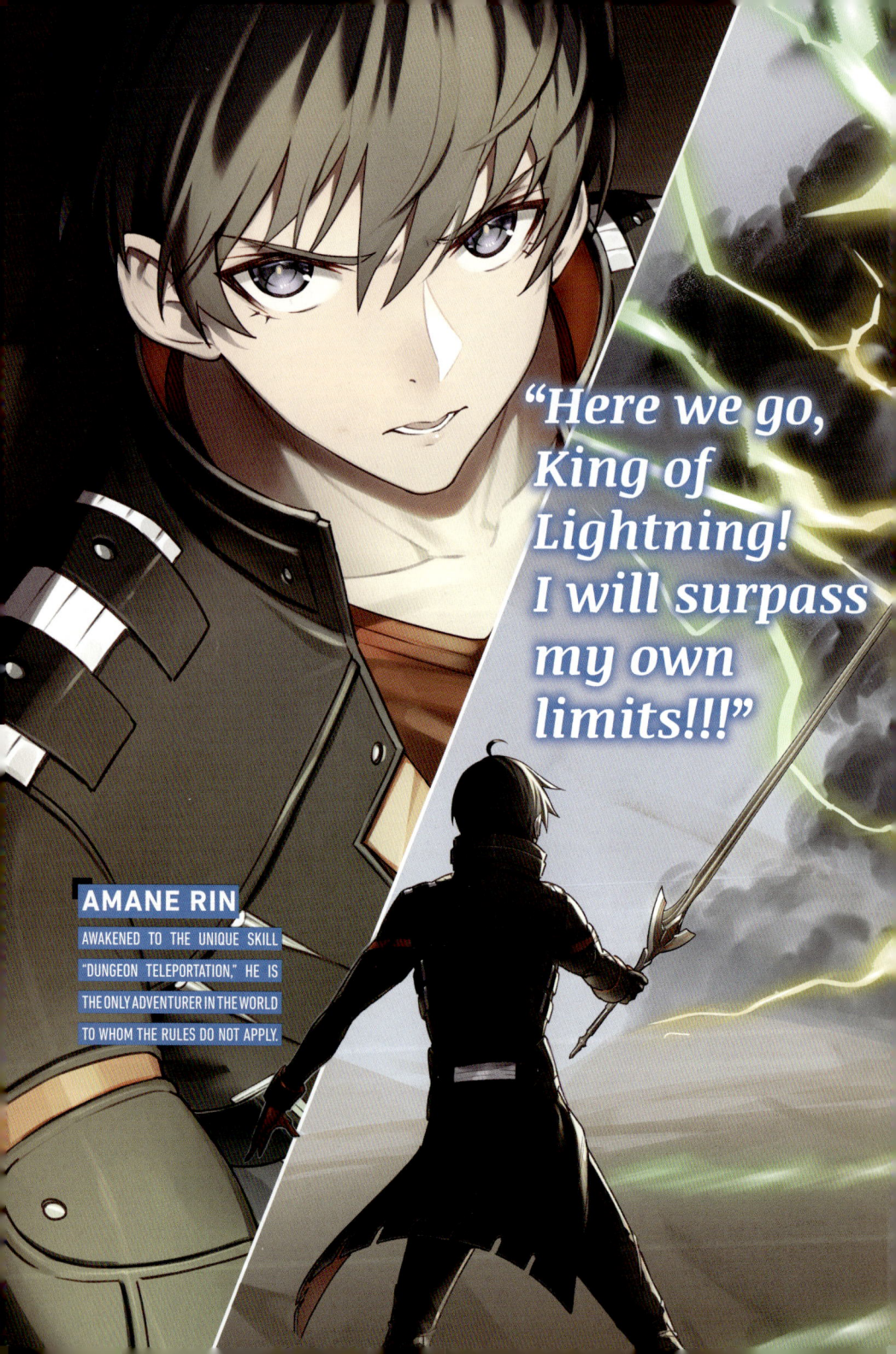

"Here we go,
King of
Lightning!
I will surpass
my own
limits!!!"

AMANE RIN
AWAKENED TO THE UNIQUE SKILL "DUNGEON TELEPORTATION," HE IS THE ONLY ADVENTURER IN THE WORLD TO WHOM THE RULES DO NOT APPLY.

LIGHTNING BEAST KING OF LIGHTNING

LEVEL: 25,000

If I couldn't overcome this lighting beast even at my best, then it was clear what I had to do. With unwavering willpower, I raised Nameless against it.

"Going solo is challenging. The fact that Rin can do it is rather unusual."

"Well, Rin-senpai is in a league of his own!"

KUROSAKI REI

A TALENTED ADVENTURER WHO SURPASSED LEVEL 500 THREE MONTHS AGO. SHE POSSESSES A UNIQUE SKILL CALLED "MAGIC SWORD." SHE PROJECTS A STOIC PERSONALITY, BUT SHE'S ACTUALLY QUITE SHY AROUND RIN.

KASAI YUI

A NOVICE HEALER-TYPE ADVENTURER WHOSE LIFE RIN SAVED INSIDE A DUNGEON. SHE BELONGS TO THE YOIZUKI GUILD.

SEKAI SAISOKU NO LEVEL UP Vol. 2
©Nagato Yamata, fame 2021
First published in Japan in 2021 by
KADOKAWA CORPORATION, Tokyo.
English translation rights arranged with
KADOKAWA CORPORATION, Tokyo.

Seven Seas press and purchase enquiries can be sent to
Marketing Manager Lianne Sentar at press@gomanga.com.
Information regarding the distribution and purchase of
digital editions is available from Digital Manager CK Russell
at digital@gomanga.com.

Follow Seven Seas Entertainment online at
sevenseasentertainment.com.

TRANSLATION: Morgan Watchorn
ADAPTATION: Nikita Greene
COVER DESIGN: Nicky Lim
LOGO DESIGN: George Panella
INTERIOR LAYOUT & DESIGN: Clay Gardner
COPY EDITOR: Meg van Huygen
PROOFREADER: Catherine Langford
LIGHT NOVEL EDITOR: Mercedez Clewis
PREPRESS TECHNICIAN: Melanie Ujimori, Jules Valera
PRODUCTION MANAGER: Lissa Pattillo
EDITOR-IN-CHIEF: Julie Davis
ASSOCIATE PUBLISHER: Adam Arnold
PUBLISHER: Jason DeAngelis

ISBN: 978-1-68579-663-1
Printed in Canada
First Printing: March 2023
10 9 8 7 6 5 4 3 2 1

THE WORLD'S FASTEST
LEVEL UP

NOVEL
2

WRITTEN BY
NAGATO
YAMATA

ILLUSTRATED BY
fame

Airship

Seven Seas Entertainment

THE WORLD'S FASTEST LEVEL UP

CONTENTS

009	PROLOGUE	
013	CHAPTER 1	DAILY LEVELING
043	CHAPTER 2	STOCK
081	CHAPTER 3	THE REMOTE MAGIC TOWER
119	INTERLUDE	TWO GIRLS IN SCHOOL UNIFORMS
123	CHAPTER 4	THE KING OF LIGHTNING
149	CHAPTER 5	BLOODLUST EATER
179	CHAPTER 6	PLUNDERER
191	CHAPTER 7	ZERO
215	EPILOGUE	
223	AFTERWORD	

PROLOGUE

A MEMORY CAME TO ME in my dreams.

It was many years ago: the people I loved were gathered together. We passed the time easily, and we were content. My younger self naively believed those halcyon days would continue forever.

Reality wasn't so generous.

Soon enough, despair rained down on us in a relentless, torrential downpour. I couldn't believe it, denied the truth of it. I could hardly face the world.

But oniichan was always there for me.

When grief or hopelessness overwhelmed me, he stayed beside me. Strangely, his quiet presence always helped guide me back from the edge. When he offered his hand, taking it was enough for me to stand again. I was so grateful to him, but at the same time, something weighed on my mind...

◆ ⌃ ◆

Amane Hana woke to the sound of energetic birds chirping outside her window. She didn't mind the wake-up call, but something nagged at her.

"Mm... I feel like I had a nostalgic dream."

She couldn't trace the exact shape of it, nor the emotionality behind it. All she remembered was a peculiar heaviness in her chest: then she'd opened her eyes and the world was sideways. The clock on her bedside table displayed thirty minutes later than her alarm was set to wake her up.

"Huh...?" A few seconds passed before every drop of blood drained from her face. "Oh, no, I'm going to be *late*!"

Amane Hana leapt out of bed and threw on her school uniform, then zoomed straight to the bathroom to wash her face and comb her long black hair. Task done, she hurried to the living room where she found her big brother, Rin. He was at the table with an empty plate in front of him. Another plate with a slice of toast sat in front of her chair.

"Morning, Hana. You're up late," he said.

"Morning—hey! If you're up this early, you should've woken *me* up!"

"It's rare of you to sleep in, so I let it slide. But hey, I made toast for you. Want it?"

"*Yeesh!* Yes, I do!"

Hana sat and shoved the toast in her mouth. No matter how much time she *didn't* have, she made sure to eat breakfast. That was just how the Amane family operated. As she ate, Rin chuckled and rose from his seat, circling the table to stand behind her.

"Oniichan?"

"You haven't tied your hair back yet. I'll do it for you."

"Mm, okay. Thanks."

Rin took the red ribbon she used to tie her hair and pulled her hair into a ponytail with familiar ease. She let him do it as if it were the most natural thing in the world.

It's been a while since he styled my hair...

Hana sank into the memories.

That embarrassed her a bit, so she turned her gaze to the TV. A news program with a few stories about dungeons was broadcasting. A new dungeon had materialized in another prefecture and high-level adventurers were being recruited to dive it first; a capable adventurer with a unique Tamer skill had died in a nearby B-rank dungeon under suspicious circumstances; and two adventurers from Japan had become S-rank—a rank with less than one hundred members across the entire world.

There was one more—Hana only paid attention to *that* news story.

"The minimum age requirement to register as an adventurer has been lowered to sixteen years of age. We've seen a rise in the number of adventurers attempting..."

My time has finally come!

Hana had made her decision about adventuring a long time ago, and now was her chance to join the fray. Her determination was set in stone.

"Okay, you're good," Rin said above her.

She gave her ponytail a brisk inspection. "Thanks, oniichan."

"Sure thing."

"Uh-oh, I'm going to be late! See you later!"

"Stay safe."

Hana shoved the last bite of her toast in her mouth and hurried out the door. Rin laughed under his breath as he saw her off.

This was one way to kick off a new day.

CHAPTER 1

DAILY LEVELING

TWENTY YEARS AGO, dungeons—supernatural labyrinths made real—suddenly spawned across the world. With them, humans gained levels, stats, and magical abilities called skills. Such things were once the domain of video games and anime, but after they entered the real world, many people became adventurers in pursuit of the fame, fortune, and special privileges the system could bring.

I, Amane Rin, was one of them. However, my motivation was different.

Thanks to a formative incident in my past, I wanted the power to protect others. It helps that I gained a unique skill called Dungeon Teleportation to assist me in my quest.

At first, people thought the ability to teleport inside dungeons was a substandard, useless skill. I might have agreed back then—but that wasn't the case anymore. Bringing the skill to LV 10 changed its conditions and revealed its true value. It allowed me to level up in a way unobtainable to others, and because of that, I leveled up faster than ever before. When disaster struck, I was strong enough to protect the people I cared about.

But I still wasn't satisfied. With my lofty goals in mind, I dove into a dungeon yet again.

Three days after the dungeon collapse at Kenzaki, the system dinged in my head.

"Dungeon takedown reward: Level increased by 2!"

"You have reached this dungeon's maximum number of allotted victories."

"Bonus Reward: Level increased by 5!"

"You will no longer receive rewards for defeating this dungeon."

I whooped. "Yeah! Now that's what I'm talking about! This makes five dungeons maxed out!"

With that, I'd added E-rank Arikawa Dungeon to my Dungeon Traveler list. Not that I knew what Dungeon Traveler *was*, beyond a title. I checked it on the status display.

> **DUNGEON TRAVELER (5/10)**
> A TITLE GRANTED TO SOMEONE WHO HAS TRAVERSED A DUNGEON IN ITS
>   ENTIRETY.
> BY TRAVELING A DUNGEON A SPECIFIC NUMBER OF TIMES, THIS PERSON
>   GAINS SPECIAL BENEFITS.

I was probably the only person in the world who knew about

this title. According to the system, it was granted to adventurers who reached the maximum number of rewards by diving a dungeon over and over—something other people were unlikely to do. What benefits would I get once I maxed out the ten dungeons I needed to complete it? I didn't have much to go on, but it was my mission to fulfill the conditions.

Defeating a dungeon started a Span that prevented me from entering another one until a week was over, but Dungeon Teleportation helped me skirt around that problem (within limits). Unfortunately, one of the activation requirements was that my destination had to be a dungeon I'd visited before. The only dungeon fulfilling that requirement was Arikawa—the dungeon I was currently in. That was why I made it my fifth target.

Three days and 148 runs later, I'd managed to do it. In the time two runs used to take me, I could now do nearly *150 runs*. It felt like no time at all when the system notified me of the dungeon's completion.

"Here's the moment I've been waiting for," I said under my breath, checking the stats display.

In those three days of grinding, I'd earned 301 levels. That had boosted my level from 3,156 to 3,457—and I'd also amassed 7,010 SP.

"As for how to delegate these skill points..."

I could boost a battle skill, but since my plan was to stick to safer dives, those kinds of skills weren't high on my priority list.

"That leaves this one."

One skill drew my eye on the display.

OBTAINED SKILLS
Dungeon Teleportation LV 12 → LV 13 (Required SP: 1,500)

DUNGEON TELEPORTATION LV 13
REQUIRED MP: 3 MP × distance (meters)
CONDITIONS: Teleportation can only occur in dungeons that have
    already been visited.
TELEPORTATION DISTANCE: Maximum 50 meters.
ACTIVATION TIME: 1 seconds × distance (meters)
SCOPE: User and user's belongings.

My unique skill, Dungeon Teleportation: a skill more important to me than any other. It was what made me special. Boosting it to LV 10 allowed my exceptional rise in levels. I predicted LV 20 would change the skill's abilities in another tremendous way. That was why, while I worked on Dungeon Traveler, I aimed to level up Dungeon Teleportation too.

I needed 2,000 SP to boost it from LV 13 to LV 14, and another 2,500 SP to go from LV 14 to LV 15. So, I deducted 6,000 SP from my total 7,010 SP to boost it to LV 15. This was the fruits of my labor:

"Dungeon Teleportation skill LV 13."

"Teleportation distance has changed."

"Maximum distance: 50 meters → Maximum distance: 100 meters."

"Dungeon Teleportation skill LV 14."

"Required MP has changed."
"3 MP × distance (meters) → 2 MP × distance (meters)."

"Dungeon Teleportation skill LV 15."
"Teleportation distance has changed."
"Maximum distance: 100 meters → Maximum distance: 200 meters."

DUNGEON TELEPORTATION LV 15

REQUIRED MP: 2 MP × distance (meters)

CONDITIONS: Teleportation can only occur in dungeons that have already been visited.

TELEPORTATION DISTANCE: Maximum 200 meters.

ACTIVATION TIME: 1 second × distance (meters)

SCOPE: User and user's belongings.

And that was about it.

"Pretty much how I expected this skill to improve."

At this point, I couldn't say whether the SP investment was worth it. Still, this skill was valuable to me, so I was determined to level it up. On the other hand, I wanted to invest in more battle skills too. Did I need to move Dungeon Teleportation further down the priority list?

"Well, this is all I can do for now."

With Arikawa fully explored, I needed five more dungeons to complete the Dungeon Traveler title. I *had* to know what benefits awaited me when I hit ten.

"I'm gonna keep that same energy tomorrow!"

And so I would have, if not for the Span.

Once I got home, I entered my room. As I sat down, I grumbled to myself, "Wait, I'm not doing *crap* tomorrow."

I was so hyped up a few hours earlier, but what could I do? That's what I got for forgetting about the Span!

With nothing else to do, I thought over my situation again. As of today, my five traveled dungeons were Shion, Arikawa, Yunagi, Yumemi, and Kenzaki. I needed another week before I could enter a new one.

"Maybe I should've dipped my toes into some other dungeons before finishing Kenzaki."

I worried I made a bad judgment call along the way. If I'd stepped a single foot in more dungeons before this, I could've completed the Dungeon Traveler title while avoiding the Span entirely.

"Not that I can do anything now. Hindsight's 20/20."

Anyway, before starting Kenzaki, I had a simple goal. Granted, I made the call under different conditions. Namely, first-time attempts of C-rank or higher dungeons granted bonus rewards, and I wanted them. Now that I was reworking my plan from the ground up, I realized I didn't need to do that again.

"The C-rank dungeons I wanted to challenge had sweet short swords and longswords as bonus rewards, but I've obtained something even better."

That *something better* was Nameless. Along with my Nameless Swordsman title, I was practically cheating when I wielded it.

My victory over the orc general was definitely thanks to this sword. I didn't need to go to dangerous dungeons to gain more swords as bonus rewards.

"It's not so bad things went this way. Thanks to all the leveling I did in Kenzaki, I can enter more dungeons now."

The Gates adventurers must pass through to enter dungeons enforced minimum level requirements, and I now qualified for higher minimums. When I pictured a scale with every opportunity I lost or won in the balance, it about weighed even.

"Guess that's enough worrying."

On that note, I had to figure out what to do for the next week.

"I'd like to farm red boars at Kenzaki and earn some money, but it collapsed...and diving a D-rank dungeon wouldn't help me level up *or* earn much at all. That's it, then. I'm taking a well-earned break!"

I'd barely spent a day above ground over the last month. No one would complain if I took an extended break here and there, so I decided to take the entire week off.

Then three days into my vacation, right when I was getting sick of endless free time, Kurosaki Rei contacted me.

AMANE RIN
LEVEL: 3,457   SP: 1,010
TITLES: Dungeon Traveler (5/10), Nameless Swordsman,
          Endbringer (Error)
HP: 27,680/27,680   MP: 6,890/6,890
ATTACK: 6,980   DEFENSE: 5,460   SPEED: 7,470
INTELLIGENCE: 4,810 RESISTANCE: 5,130 LUCK: 4,720

SKILLS: Dungeon Teleportation LV 15, Enhanced Strength LV MAX, Herculean Strength LV MAX, Superhuman Strength LV 3, High-speed Movement LV MAX, Gale Wind LV 3, Mana Boost LV 2, Mana Recovery LV 2, Enemy Detection LV 4, Evasion LV 4, Status Condition Resistance LV 4, Appraisal, Item Box LV 5

The day after Rei contacted me, I met her at a café near my house. We'd picked the spot because she lived in the neighborhood as well. Once I entered, I found Rei was already there.

"Rin, over here!" she called.

"Sorry, did you wait long?"

"No, I just got here."

Oh. That *was* how I was supposed to answer that question back then. The exchange I'd had when Yui was late finally made sense.

"I apologize for texting you out of the blue. Did I catch you during a bad time?" she asked.

"No, you're good. I was actually thinking I wanted to see you too." There were a lot of things I needed to check up on. I was glad she gave me an opportunity to ask.

"O-oh! That's fine, then," she answered.

Her cheeks flushed a little red. I questioningly raised an eyebrow at her. Did she have a slight cold or something? While I wanted to ask, I set it aside for more pressing priorities.

Once the waiter took our orders, I started asking questions.

"Did you talk to Kazami and the rest of the Kings of Unique since then?"

"Just yesterday. That's why I called you here, in fact."

"Mind if I ask how they reacted?"

"To what, specifically?"

"I'm most curious what they thought after hearing they defeated the orc general... I hope they don't get a big head and wrap you up in more trouble."

Kazami's party was always prideful, so I was concerned how they'd act once they knew they'd defeated a higher-level monster. I couldn't stand the thought of their heads swelling any bigger over such a sloppy success story. On top of that, I was the one who decided to attribute the victory to them. It was my responsibility to make sure they didn't get cocky and full of themselves.

That's why Rei's reply completely blindsided me.

"I doubt that'll be an issue. The party disbanded."

"Disbanded...?" I tilted my head, uncomprehending.

Rei continued. "Kazami-san talked to us yesterday. He felt guilty for endangering the party and didn't think he deserved to lead us anymore, so he disbanded the party."

"*Kazami* said that?"

I never would've pegged Kazami for the remorseful type, but Rei nodded her agreement.

Ever since Kazami gained his unique skill and became an adventurer a year ago, danger was a foreign concept to him. Did the collapse give him a reality check about how dangerous dungeons

could be? Since he ultimately defeated the orc general (or so we told him), I worried he would get over that fear pretty quickly.

Despite that, every detail Rei gave compounded the impression that the events during the dungeon collapse had discouraged Kazami from further reckless behavior. It was way more than I predicted—or expected.

"After he disbanded us, he questioned whether we truly defeated the orc general," Rei said.

"Wait, what do you mean?"

"Kazami-san felt how vastly outmatched he was. He'd expelled every ounce of his magic, so he didn't seem convinced that he could defeat it, even with my explanation."

"I see."

Kazami tended to put too much stock in his own ideas, but he wasn't stupid. If he pulled his head out of the sand and thought things through, the conclusion he arrived at would be obvious. Of course, the problem with his theory was that someone *else* would've had to defeat the orc general.

"He doesn't have any idea who really defeated it, does he?" I asked.

"No. The boss room door wouldn't have opened unless we all died. But if there was one exception to that..."

Rei looked at me directly. I shook my head.

"He might speculate, but he knows my strength. I doubt he'd think I had the power to pop in and save the day. Too convenient."

"You're right, he didn't. In the end, he accepted he was the one who did it, but he chalked it up to luck. Since Kazami created the whole mess, he didn't think he had the right to lead a party anymore."

"So he disbanded the group. Huh. Did the others accept the explanation?"

"Yeah. The incident was a devastating blow to us."

"Yeah, I guess it would be..."

At first, this seemed like an unexpected reaction from the overconfident Kings of Unique. Reflecting on it, maybe it *was* in line for them.

Dungeons first appeared twenty years ago: at first, only a few brave people haphazardly explored their depths. Over time, information spread for more cautious adventurers to utilize in their adventures. And most importantly, we developed methods to dive *safely*. Irregularities, like when I unexpectedly encountered the Nameless Knight, were rare—exceptionally rare.

Most adventurers, regardless of rank, worked with safety in mind, so danger remained at bay. How many people *actually* knew how scary dungeons could be from firsthand experience? How many people found out and *still* chose to enter them?

In the end, Kazami's party made an understandable decision after drawing so close to the brink of death. I didn't know whether they'd continue on as adventurers, but I knew they were thankful to be alive to rethink their paths in life.

That brought up another question.

"If they disbanded, that leaves you on your own. Have you decided what you'll do next?" Would she continue adventuring or quit it altogether? I really wanted to know her decision.

"I'm going to continue. That said, I decided on a new goal," she replied.

"What goal?"

"Ah, it's a secret." Rei's face reddened again. Was she embarrassed? I was curious, but it would be rude to force an answer from her.

"Well, don't push yourself too hard, you hear?" I said.

"I won't."

The mien of her expression turned melancholy, as if, in some way, she'd given up on something. I couldn't put my finger on it.

Maybe I should've invited her to form a party with me, although practically, I couldn't. Dungeon Teleportation only worked on me: plus, our significant level gap also meant she would hold me back. We both knew it.

Unspoken words hung in the air between us like cold fog. Then Rei broke the silence by reaching for her bag and pulling something out.

"I almost forgot. This is for you, Rin."

"What is it?"

She handed me five envelopes. One of them was about half as thick as the others. If this was what I thought it was, then...

"Rei, this isn't—"

"Yes, it's money. It's 4.5 million yen, to be precise."

"Wait, wait, wait. Why are you giving me this?! This is a terrifying amount of cash!"

I panicked and pushed the envelopes back toward her, but she slid them back insistently.

"Let me explain," she said. "You used advanced-level health recovery potions on us that day, which cost a minimum of one million yen each. I'm simply returning the value of what you used on us."

I nodded in understanding, yet another thing nagged at me.

"I get wanting to repay me, but why do you have enough for *all* of you? None of the others know I was there. Don't tell me you're trying to front the cost."

"I'm not. As the only conscious person, I told them they were my potions. They gave the money to me first."

"Got it. Guess that makes sense."

They'd taken enough damage to knock them out—so they couldn't argue much with her explanation. Besides, they were successful adventurers, so a measly million yen probably didn't make a dent in their savings. Except for one envelope, which was half a million short.

"I'm sorry, but half is all I can pay for now," Rei explained. "I'll pay back the rest soon. Please give me a bit of time."

Ah, I knew it.

Frankly, I didn't want any financial compensation. I was the one who chose to heal them. Nonetheless, after hearing her serious explanation and seeing her half-full envelope, it felt rude to refuse her.

I took a breath and accepted the envelopes. "Okay. I'll take it."

"Thanks, Rin."

"It feels weird being thanked for this, but you're welcome."

With that settled, we turned to more enjoyable conversation.

A half-hour later, we decided to split. Before we did, though, Rei nervously piped up with something else.

"Listen, Rin. If it's okay with you, I'd like to go to another dungeon together sometime."

"That *does* sound fun."

Our levels and goals were pretty disparate, but I thought it would be a good time regardless. So, on that positive note, we said our goodbyes.

"See you next time, Rei."

"Yeah. Bye, Rin."

We turned away from each other and went in opposite directions. I looked at the blue sky and wondered when our paths would cross next.

A few days later, the Span ended. *Finally!*

The first thing I did was visit some dungeons I'd never entered before. That way, I cleared the condition I needed to use Dungeon Teleportation to bypass my next Span.

The ones within reasonable distance from home—which also had level limits that I qualified for—included four E-rank dungeons, four D-rank dungeons, and three C-rank dungeons. Adventurers weren't allowed to use their abilities around town except for during emergencies, so I had to use public transportation to visit them. Thanks to that inconvenience, I spent two long days reaching ten of them. The eleventh was a C-rank dungeon I saved for last.

The next day, I made it to that C-rank dungeon—Marou Dungeon. As an intermediate-class dungeon with a recommended level of 2,000, the minimum level requirement to pass through the gate was level 1,000. The reason for the difference between the two numbers was simple: a high-difficulty dungeon had lots of floors. The deeper I went, the higher-level monsters I'd encounter. Basically, an adventurer at level 1,000 could beat monsters on the shallow floors, but that number wouldn't fly on the deepest ones.

The reason I saved Marou for last was its bonus reward for first-time challengers, but there *were* more requirements than that. I got pre-annoyed just thinking about it.

"No point putting it off."

Trying to stay enthusiastic, I entered Marou's depths.

About ten minutes later, I encountered the first monster. It was a meter-tall wolf with red fur—a fire wolf.

FIRE WOLF
LEVEL: 1,200
A wolf-type monster with fire-resistant fur. It's known for its nimbleness and ability to breathe fire.

This fire wolf had the most unusual characteristics of the monsters I'd fought to date. It snarled and immediately launched a fireball at me.

I quickly stepped out of range. "*Oof*, you don't waste time, do ya?"

The fireball slammed into the wall behind me, where a chunk turned to ash and crumbled. Was it using magic or some other innate fire ability? It wasn't quite like the magic skills we adventurers used, but the results were basically identical. I hadn't fought many opponents with magic. They inevitably forced me into a ranged battle, which my stats weren't optimized for.

If this wolf was a human sorcerer, I could rely on speed and close the distance, but that didn't work on monsters. Many of them had more than magic—they had claws, teeth, and brute strength to fall back on.

More enemies like this would pave my path to the top. I couldn't avoid them forever: I needed to fight them and develop my own way of dealing with them.

"Now!"

As tricky as a ranged magic user was for me, this fire wolf was only a third of my total level. The flames startled me at first, but once I calmed down and analyzed the situation, it was a manageable threat.

The fire wolf launched another burst of fire, which created an opening I could take advantage of with my speed. I struck it once with Nameless. The fire wolf gurgled as I lopped its head off and rolled away as its body collapsed.

"Easy victory, I guess," I murmured to myself. I bent over to harvest the magic stone from the corpse and saw it was transparent. My shoulders drooped. "Figures I wouldn't get lucky and find the rare magic stone on the first try."

Depending on the type of wolf I encountered in the dungeon,

they might possess a rare magic stone. A fire wolf could contain a red magic stone imbued with fire mana. Rare magic stones—like the one that might be inside a fire wolf—sold for high prices, but I wasn't searching for a profit. I needed rare stones to fulfill the bonus reward's second condition.

This dungeon spawned magic wielding wolf-type monsters called, obviously enough, magic wolves. Nine types existed, and I needed to collect rare magic stones from each one, which meant a frustrating day of grinding for random drops.

"I think my intel said getting one was a one-in-fifty chance. It's a long road ahead..."

Ugh. Doing the math, I'd have to beat about five hundred wolves to guarantee I got them all. Nothing to do but move forward, blade in hand.

"...And this makes one hundred!"

Nameless sank through the neck of my hundredth magic wolf. I'd obtained the red stone on my fortieth felled fire wolf. After that, I turned my attention to slaughtering earth wolves. The magic stone I withdrew from lucky wolf number one hundred was an earthen brown.

"Eureka!"

Two rare types of magic stones down—and seven to go. Acquiring them burned through an hour and a half of the day. At this rate, it would be over six hours before I collected all nine.

"Most people would collect these with a full party. There's no time limit, but I'd better hustle if I don't want to be down here for eternity."

With the red and brown stones handled, fighting any fire wolves or earth wolves in my path was a waste of time. I needed to work smarter, not harder.

"Enemy Detection ought to do it."

The detection radius flared. Two floors down, five water wolves lurked in a pack. Five at once would be a handful, but beggars couldn't be choosers.

"Dungeon Teleportation!"

A few dozen seconds passed. The skill activated, and as I appeared two floors down, I launched a surprise attack. They didn't see me coming—and I took full advantage of that. I beheaded two wolves before they could so much as scent me. The dying wolves yelped while the others snarled in retaliation. Two of the surviving wolves fired at me with water lasers.

"Too late!"

I dodged their counterattack easily and slipped into close proximity, where I slashed at their vulnerable stomachs and necks. They growled as they went down. The last one caught me defenseless, so it launched at my open left side with its greedy maw wide open.

"Just kidding~"

I summoned my Kirikuji Short Sword from Item Box into my left hand and sliced upward. Compared to Nameless, it didn't offer much attack boost, but my stats had my back. The blade easily dug in and severed the water wolf's jaw. It made a startled, wet yip of pain. I followed up the damage by striking it with Nameless, which finished it off.

Out of the magic stones I collected from the five bodies, one glittered blue.

"Dang, *seriously*?! It only took five to get it, and it's hefty too!"

This significantly decreased the total number of magic wolves due for a date with my sword. Not that I was in for easy battles, but silver linings or whatever. Plus, knowing I could fight five at once, I could cut back on time.

"Using Enemy Detection and Dungeon Teleportation over such a wide area drains my MP, but the strategy itself yields good results. I'll switch to more local Enemy Detection and go from there," I said to myself, activating Enemy Detection once again.

The hunt progressed nicely. I managed to loot three more rare magic stones from wind wolves, light wolves, and dark wolves without too much trouble. Several minutes after snagging a dark magic stone, a poison wolf with vivid purple fur appeared in front of me.

POISON WOLF

LEVEL: 1,400

A wolf-type monster with purple fur. It's known for its nimbleness and ability to breath poison. Poison affliction inflicts 1% damage to HP per minute.

"You're here at last!"

This monster had the ability to inflict a status condition. It was unusual, even among monsters that wielded magic. In some ways, status conditions could get several times deadlier than normal attack-stat-based magic.

The poison wolf growled. I huffed in alarm as it unleashed a breath of poison mist in my direction. At base, it had no attack power, but contact with that would inflict the poison status if I was unlucky.

"My defense and Status Condition Resistance skill *should* make the probability of poisoning low, but I'd rather not risk it."

Just because it wasn't likely didn't mean the chance was zero. The odds were something like 1 percent—but even a level 1 adventurer's poison magic might work on a level 1,000 monster. I'd stored poison antidotes in my Item Box, but like health potions, I couldn't use them in quick succession. In this battle, there was no room to let my guard down.

"When it comes to defeating this thing while mitigating the risks..."

Once the poison cloud drifted away, the wolf still didn't approach me. The most advantageous position was *away* from the poisoned area, but given my fighting style, distance was infeasible. Undoubtedly, the poison wolf wanted me to expose myself to the poison and close the distance.

My best strategy was obvious.

"Dungeon Teleportation!"

I teleported behind the poison wolf. The poison mist was in front of it, not behind it. When the poison wolf noticed me, it made a startled sound.

"Ha! Too late."

I arced Nameless down and bisected the poison wolf's body—a one-hit kill.

"Subjugation complete. Now for the magic stone."

I harvested the stone, but it was transparent. Not unexpected for poison wolf number one.

"Nothing to sulk over. Onward!"

I set out in search of my next prey. The kills and harvests went smoothly until I progressed from poison wolves to paralysis wolves to sleep wolves. Eventually, I obtained each species' rare magic stones.

Finally, I had the full spread of nine—which meant it was time to descend to the last floor.

"All that's left is to beat the boss," I mused as I reached the boss room on Marou's thirtieth floor. As a little bonus of wolf hunting, I'd gained two levels on the way there.

No one was already fighting the boss, so I strode straight past the boss room doors. Once inside, a giant ash-colored wolf stood before me, looming at two entire meters tall.

Marou's boss: a king wolf. Level 2,000.

As is, the king wolf didn't use magic. It was nothing more

than a monster with high physical abilities. Of course, it wasn't the boss I wanted to defeat.

"Eat up," I told it, throwing all nine magic stones—red, brown, blue, green, white, black, purple, pink, and yellow—his way. The king wolf snarled but eyed the stones as if it was waiting for them to be tossed its way—before devouring the magic stones with its fanged, slavering mouth.

As it absorbed the abilities of the other wolves, its coat began to gleam with the nine colors of the stones.

RAINBOW KING WOLF
LEVEL: 3,000
A wolf-like monster with multicolored fur in a lustrous range of nine shades. It possesses agility unprecedented for its large frame and attacks with a variety of magic.

This was what I wanted to fight. The locals called it the gaming wolf. When Marou first spawned, it was overflowing with adventurers who wanted the rare magic stones. For the dungeon takedown reward, anyone who beat the boss would gain forty levels and a ring that granted zero effects. The lackluster rewards didn't match up with the dungeon's overall difficulty level, which lessened the appeal, so most people skipped beating the dungeon itself.

But one day, when a random party was fighting the king wolf for the first time, one of their members dropped their rare magic stone. To everyone's surprise, the king wolf gobbled up the stone and transformed itself into a Wind King Wolf. Once they defeated it, it dropped the usual ring, except the ring had a wind-attribute attached to it! They discovered that equipping the ring granted the adventurer a 15 percent decrease in wind-type damage.

After that, tons of other parties experimented with other types of magic stones to see how the king wolf would evolve. They collectively concluded that defeating the boss with attributes from any given stone rewarded them with a ring that decreased damage from those attributes by 15 percent.

I wanted a Ring of Marou with *all nine* attributes. That was why I now stared down the Rainbow King Wolf. If I could defeat it, my day of grinding would be absolutely worth it.

Unfortunately, as the battle unfolded, I realized something.

"Shoot. This is a bad matchup..." I muttered.

First, the Rainbow King Wolf was slightly lower level than I was, which nullified Nameless's stat-boost effects. Moreover, swapping from melee to ranged combat was pretty complicated.

The wolf growled and launched a fireball—and I dodged too late. It struck me in the shoulder.

"Argh!"

The damage wasn't much, but *dang*, was it hot! Ugh! No time to fixate on the pain. If I stumbled and flinched from one attack, the wolf would launch another volley of magic.

"This is only going to get worse if I keep dodging magic and looking for openings... I need to commit to something, and quick!"

I activated my Gale Wind and Superhuman Strength skills simultaneously.

> Superhuman Strength LV 3: +30% to attack (COSTS 10 MP PER SECOND)
> Gale Wind LV 3: +30% to speed (COSTS 10 MP PER SECOND)

This fight wouldn't last much longer. I'd push the battle into the climax right here and now!

"Here we go!"

After a moment to focus, I kicked into high gear and sped up, deftly dodging magic attacks as I went. My goal: close the gap between me and the enemy. The Rainbow King Wolf roared at my approach—it wasn't going to just roll over and show me its belly. It launched fireball, a roaring gale of wind, and more, show-casing the colorful array of its magic. I dodged everything. Maybe it recognized its onslaught wasn't working, because it changed tactics to spewing fire into the air between us.

Just as I anticipated!

"No second-guessing!" I shouted to pump myself up. My speed increased.

Superhuman Strength and Gale Wind steadily drained my mana, but they lessened the impact of the fiercely licking flames. As long as it only lasted a short time, I could endure the burn! I was after success, not a full HP bar. I sacrificed 1,000 HP to storm through the wall of fire. The Rainbow King Wolf drew a breath as if to unleash another stream of magic—

"Oh, no, you *don't*!"

I threw an Exploding Stone into the Rainbow King Wolf's open mouth, and true to its name, it went off with a solid *boom*. The explosion hit the wolf like a ton of bricks; it howled in pain. Glad I stocked up on Exploding Stones like I stockpiled health recovery potions.

The abrupt internal damage sent the wolf into a frenzy. Time to double down!

"You better not think I'm done!"

With my prey within range, *I* was the wolf at the door. I swung Nameless with a grunt and sliced the wolf open between its leg and belly. Fast, sharp, and precise—this was my chance to grasp victory!

Thirty more seconds. I predicted each bout of magic and evaded accordingly, landing hits in between. And at last—

"Here comes the final blow!"

The Rainbow King Wolf grew sluggish from its injuries, so I seized my chance to strike a massive blow. The weight of the hit reverberated down the hilt in my hands as the blade severed the Rainbow King Wolf's head from its body.

At the same time, the system chimed to alert my victory.

"You have defeated the final boss."

"Gained XP: Level increased by 5!"

"Dungeon takedown reward: Level increased by 40!"

"Whew...it's over."

All the rewards combined gave me a total of forty-five levels gained. Since the boss I defeated was simply an evolved version of the basic king wolf, I hadn't done anything to trigger an extra boss or change the basic level-up reward. That part was a shame.

Still, I had plenty to be happy about.

"I got the item I wanted! *Yes!!!*"

I picked up the bonus item—the Ring of Marou (True)—and used appraisal on it.

RING OF MAROU (TRUE)

A bonus item given to those who defeat the Rainbow King Wolf
upon challenging Marou Dungeon for the first time.

RECOMMENDED EQUIP LEVEL: 3,000

Reduces damage from fire, water, wind, earth, light, and dark
magic by 15%.

Decreases the probability of poison, paralysis, and sleep
conditions by 15%.

"Sweet! Exactly like the information said! This is a nicely powerful item."

An overpowered weapon like Nameless muddied the numbers, but any item that boosted stats by 10 percent, or even granted a 10 percent reduction in damage, was an item anyone would covet. Among such items, 15 percent magic damage reduction to *everything* made the Ring of Marou (True) extremely valuable.

"This item is so good, people say that ever since the day it was discovered, even adventurers over level 10,000 spend weeks preparing to obtain it. I'm glad I got my hands on it."

But there was a problem.

"This ring is so oversized, it'll slide right off...whoa!"

The second I slipped it onto the middle finger of my left hand, the ring automatically changed size to a perfect fit.

"Huh, that's a magic item for you. I don't usually equip accessory-type items, so I kinda forgot they could do this."

I got back down to business. "Still something else to do..."

I pulled the nine glittering magic stones from the Rainbow King Wolf's corpse and tucked the hide into my Item Box. The hide made for good armor material: It would sell for a high price.

The teleportation spell began to activate.

"Phew. Glad I didn't run into any Nameless Knights again..." I muttered. I let out a sigh of relief as I put Marou—and my victory—behind me.

"Dungeon takedown reward: Level increased by 40!"
"Level: 4,074 → 4,114"
"Dungeon takedown reward: Level increased by 40!"
"Level: 4,314 → 4,354."
"Dungeon takedown reward: Level increased by 40!"
"Level: 4,754 → 4,794."

The day after I defeated Marou, I used Dungeon Teleportation to do some rapid leveling. I was a pro at looping dungeon runs at this point, so I went hard. On my first and second runs, I stayed on my toes while I fought the king wolves. Every time after that was a walk in the park. After the fifth run, they went down with one strike from Nameless. A few days later—at just over forty runs—I reached the moment I was waiting for. The system alert in my head rang out, and I knew I'd maxed out Marou.

"You have reached this dungeon's maximum number of allotted victories."

"Bonus Reward: Level increased by 80!"

"You will no longer receive rewards for defeating this dungeon."

"Oh, it's over?" I said. "This one went smoothly, and forty levels over about forty runs gave me a *massive* level boost."

Not to mention the stack of SP I scored. I used it to boost Superhuman Strength from LV 3 to LV 5, Gale Wind from LV 3 to LV 5, and Dungeon Teleportation from LV 15 to LV 16. The last one barely moved the activation time from 1 second to 0.8 seconds, but even a small decrease in the activation helped. Depending on the situation, it could become more useful in battle.

My enthusiastic leveling left me with 6,000 extra SP, but I was in no hurry to use it. It was nice to have a stockpile to figure out another day. Right now, I had other things to take care of.

"Heck yeah! I'm going to shoot my levels into the sky like I'm rocketing to space!" I shouted.

No one was around to hear my enthusiasm. I could feel my jets sputter.

AMANE RIN

LEVEL: 5,154   **SP:** 6,010

TITLES: Dungeon Traveler (6/10), Nameless Swordsman,
    Endbringer (Error)

HP: 40,860/40,860   **MP:** 10,680/10,680

ATTACK: 10,030   **DEFENSE:** 8,260   **SPEED:** 10,670

INTELLIGENCE: 7,630   **RESISTANCE:** 7,730   **LUCK:** 7,220

SKILLS: Dungeon Teleportation LV 16, Enhanced Strength LV MAX,
    Herculean Strength LV MAX, Superhuman Strength LV 5,
    High-speed Movement LV MAX, Gale Wind LV 5, Mana Boost LV 2,
    Mana Recovery LV 2, Enemy Detection LV 4, Evasion LV 4,
    Status Condition Resistance LV 4, Appraisal, Item Box LV 5

SWORD OF THE NAMELESS KNIGHT

A sword used by the Nameless Knight.

RECOMMENDED EQUIP LEVEL: 5,000

ATTACK +5,000

When an enemy (human or monster) is of a higher level than the
    wielder, all parameters except HP and MP increase by 40% each.

CHAPTER 2

STOCK

T HE DAY AFTER I maxed out Marou, I chatted over breakfast with Hana.

"Oniichan, are you free this weekend?" she asked me.

As a solo dungeon diver, I was free to control my own schedule as I wished. I nodded without hesitation. "Sure, I should be able to fit something in."

"Great! Make sure you wear an outfit that's comfortable to move in."

"Uh, sure. Okay?"

Was this going to be the triathlon version of carrying her shopping bags or something? I couldn't think of anything else it would be, but then a few days later, we arrived at a dungeon. A *dungeon*, of all things!

"Why are we *here*?!" I exclaimed.

"Yikes! Don't shout right next to me, oniichan. You scared me!"

Wait, wait, wait! There was no way I *wouldn't* have this reaction. I mean, she brought me to Sumifuku—an E-rank dungeon.

Like Shion, it was a low-level, beginner-friendly dungeon. I'd set foot inside it as a potential easy dungeon to max out for my Dungeon Traveler title.

"Hana, *why* are we at a dungeon?" I pressed, suspicious.

"What, I didn't tell you?"

"You did not."

"Sorry! So, here's the thing..."

Hana started at the beginning and explained herself.

Considering the dangers of dungeons, the global standard age limit for entering dungeons was sixteen or above. Public outcry rose last year pressuring Japan—which required adventurers to be at least eighteen—to lower the age limit. Since a nation's strongest adventurers essentially dictated their global status, they caved and lowered the limit to seventeen last year. This year, they lowered it to sixteen to match the global standard.

Of course, age wasn't the single requirement to start dungeon diving. Everyone had to earn their adventurer qualifications through the Dungeon Association's training course. I took my course right out of high school, but now that students could pursue their qualifications, they were actively recruiting within high schools.

Based on her explanation, the Dungeon Association had recruited *Hana*. I supposed that was fine, but I didn't let her off the hook yet.

"Okay, but why ask me to come? Won't you take the course and get your qualifications *before* entering a dungeon? Besides, where is this sudden adventuring urge coming from?"

"People who go through the school take a simplified course and get their provisional qualifications. The Dungeon Association is sending someone to guide us through a real dungeon today, but anyone who feels anxious about it is allowed to bring an adventurer they know."

"Hmm. I see." So she'd asked me, someone she trusted. "You should've told me first. What if I was stuck in the middle of a Span?" I said.

"What's a Span?"

She looked like she'd never heard the term before. Had that course taught her *anything*?!

"Forget that pointless stuff! The participants are supposed to gather over there," she said as she grabbed my hand. "Hurry up, oniichan!"

"Yeah, yeah. I get it."

Hana dragged me over. I sighed and followed her to the gathering spot, where around three hundred students stood surrounded by people who looked a lot like guards.

"Quite the turnout," I observed.

"They must've recruited from more than one school," Hana replied.

"That would explain it." Visiting several high schools seemed like an effective way to snag these kinds of numbers.

Someone dressed in a Dungeon Association uniform spoke over the crowd, which gradually quieted down.

"I'm going to do a roll call for all participants in this practice drill. Once you hear your name, please line up here and show

your stats to the guard accompanying you! Name and level only
are fine!"

"Crap!"

I froze. Hearing that, I'd accidentally let the word slip out.

"Oniichan, what's wrong?"

"N-nothing."

"Don't be weird. Let's just go over there!"

"Uh, right."

I followed after her, but on the inside, I was sweating bullets.
If I showed my stats, people would find out my level was over
5,000—and it wasn't hard to imagine the drama if that number
got out. Revealing my level was a slippery slope to sharing the
secrets behind Dungeon Teleportation.

This was bad, but I couldn't abandon my sister.

What should I do...?

A bright idea hit me. "Hana, wait just a second. I need to pull
up my stats display."

"Okay."

I hurriedly scrolled through my list of unobtained skills in
search of one in particular. In a few seconds, I found it.

NEW SKILL
Conceal LV 1 (SP NEEDED: 5,000)

"Found it."

Conceal was an advanced skill, and with a cost of 5,000 SP,
it was more expensive than any of the others I'd obtained so far.

As pricey an investment as it was, it would do one thing alone: give me the ability to overwrite my status information.

Obviously, it wouldn't do anything like actually rewrite my attack power to a figure ten times what it was. The point of the skill was instead to change what other people *saw*.

Normally, when showing their status, an adventurer had three options of what to display.

Name only.

Name and level only.

Name and skills only.

It wasn't possible to hide only part of that information. For example, if I was level 1,000, I couldn't hide one zero and make myself look like I was level 100. If I knew Enhanced Strength and novice magic skills, I couldn't hide Enhanced Strength and only show the magic skills. But the Conceal skill made such trickery possible.

A savvy mind would see the danger in that immediately. Conceal users could create a fake stat display and deceive people for personal gain—things like infiltrating lower-level parties to steal their items or inflating their levels to leech off stronger ones. Because of such possible scams, using Conceal was banned.

That said, there was no way to prove who *had* Conceal, so it wasn't a full-fledged crime to learn it. But *doing* something that required Conceal got adventurers slapped with punishments way beyond normal ones.

In my position, using it wouldn't harm anyone, so it was a bit of a moral gray area.

"Looks like I'm getting it," I told myself.

I paid the 5,000 SP and learned Conceal. It was a bunch of SP to instantly burn through, but nowadays, I could recover that in one day. I didn't need to overthink it.

The one problem left was what level to pretend I was. Just the other day, I'd beaten Marou, which had a 1,000-level minimum. I could hide that from my history, but my record would still say I'd been there. To be safe, my level needed to be 1,000 at a minimum, so I set it right above that.

"Oniichan, are you done yet?" Hana called.

"Be right there," I replied, surreptitiously overwriting my display. Together, we went to see the Dungeon Association rep. A man in his forties, he was the same person who'd spoken to the crowd earlier. He noticed us approach.

"Nice to meet you, I'm Katagiri," he said. "I'm from the Dungeon Association's Promotional Department. May I have your names?"

"I'm Amane Hana. Nice to meet you too. And this is..."

"Amane Rin," I supplied. "I'll be escorting her today."

"May I see your stats?"

"Of course."

I showed him my doctored stats screen with my name and level displayed. Katagiri-san checked it over and nodded.

"Thank you. You're about to enter an E-rank dungeon, so that level should be plenty. If anything happens, I'm over level 7,000. Don't you worry."

"That's reassuring," I replied.

Katagiri-san smiled gently. "And I won't be the only Association member here. We have a lot of youngsters this time around, but they're all C-rank with proven abilities, so they've got the job covered. Our most promising among them is...oh! Perfect timing. Yanagi, come on over here!"

A passing young man with brown hair turned and approached us. "Y-yes? What is it?" he asked hesitantly.

"I wanted to introduce you to these two," Katagiri-san said, then faced us. "This is Yanagi. He's a fresh college grad with a regular job, but he's a talented adventurer with a level over 5,000. He'll dive with us."

Yanagi-san gave off a timid first impression, but he still dipped his head at us in greeting. "H-hi, I'm Yanagi. I'm glad to be working with you today."

"Likewise. We're looking forward to it."

He offered his hand, and I accepted the handshake. He had a firm grip; exactly what I'd expect from someone at his level, even if it didn't match his personality.

"Hmm," Yanagi hummed, as if contemplating something.

"Is something wrong?" I asked.

"N-no, it's nothing! All good here!"

He released my hand in a panic. I had a feeling it wasn't *nothing*, but I didn't like pushing when people clammed up. We parted without fanfare.

A few minutes later, Hana went to change with the other participants into the equipment provided by the Association. Wow, the rows of neatly prearranged armor was a far cry from the fat

pile of *nothing* I got during *my* time...wait. Was I too young to complain about kids these days?

While they changed, I swapped into my equipment just in case. I used Item Box to do it instantly.

Once everyone finished changing, we headed into Sumifuku.

"Dungeon Teleportation," I whispered, timing it so it seemed like I passed through the Gate the normal way. After all, I was still subject to the Span.

Inside Sumifuku, they moved us to an open space. There, Katagiri-san began to explain the process.

"Okay, everyone. We're going to have you challenge a monster and see if you get your stats. As you've heard, defeating your first monster is the only way to obtain them, and only 10 percent of people will manage it."

The students' voices bubbled up like boiling water as they whispered amongst themselves.

"It's really true only some of us will get stats? I'm scared now..."

"I came all the way here. I'd better get them!"

"Come on, unique skill! Gimme a unique skill!"

The atmosphere was tense, which made sense. The next few minutes would define the course their lives.

I glanced beside me, where Hana had clasped her hands together. She shook nervously. I placed a hand on hers.

"Oniichan?"

"Whether or not you'll gain stats is total chance, so there's no reason to get your hopes up. Or is that that too blunt of me to say...?"

This might've been the wrong way to comfort her. So I thought, until Hana snorted a laugh.

"What the heck?" she said. "If you're going to comfort me, you should commit to it!"

"S-sorry."

"It's fine. You helped me relax a little. Thanks."

Like she said, her expression relaxed. I was relieved I eased her nerves, but I had my own concerns. She never told me about wanting to become an adventurer. I thought about asking her about her goals, but before I could, Katagiri-san resumed his explanation.

"We'll send one escort per three participants to defeat their monsters. Any remaining participants will stay here on standby. Those with companions of D-rank or higher may choose to go alone with them. Those of you who obtain stats are required to return and report to me."

I made a sound of confirmation and nodded. "That means you need to choose whether you want an Association member to come with us or if you want to go alone with me," I asked Hana. "Which do you prefer?"

"Umm, I don't think I want a stranger to watch me. Let's go together!"

"All right, let's get to it then."

With our plan confirmed, we separated from the group and left to hunt a monster. From what I could tell, about half of the participants chose the same option.

A few minutes into our walk together, we found exactly what we were searching for.

"Oniichan, is that what I think it is?" Hana asked.

"Yeah. It looks pretty different from the smiling ones you see in video games, but you're spot on."

A transparent creature in the shape of an eyeless, noseless blob—a slime—awaited us. I used Appraisal on it.

> **LESSER SLIME**
> **LEVEL:** 1
> A monster with a transparent, liquid-like body and minimal Attack power. It can be killed by destroying the nucleus—or core—at the center of its body.

I examined the results of Appraisal and said, "Level one, huh? This should be easy for you, Hana."

Slimes came in many shapes and abilities, but a basic lesser slime was similar to the kind of weak monster that popped up in the first levels of RPGs. They went down easy. Extremely powerful types of slimes existed too—ones with random special abilities such as blast slimes, which exploded on contact with any hostile attacker, or kraken slimes, which the rumors said were nasty sorts that melted the armor (all of their clothes, really) off of girls.

"Oniichan, why are you looking at the ceiling?"

Hana brought me back to reality in a snap. "No reason," I said, and changed the subject immediately. "You better take down this slime quick. See that red orb in the center of its body? That's the magic stone that serves as the slime's core. Destroy it and you'll defeat it."

"O-okay! I'll give it a try!"

Hana gripped the knife she received from the Dungeon Association and approached the slime on shaky legs. Slimes were so weak that even an average joe without stats could kill one, but she was extra careful from the fear of her first monster kill. She stopped in front of the slime and slowly, carefully angled her knife.

"Take this!" she shouted, forcing the knife down and striking the core. A second later, the slime exploded with a *pop*. Slimes left no materials and no magic stones, so they weren't exactly prized among adventurers.

I waited tensely. Everything boiled down to this moment. I raised my eyebrows at Hana. Had she obtained her stats?

Hana's eyes went wide with surprise.

"'Stats obtained?' A voice in my head said something about 'XP obtained' and 'leveled up!'"

Hana was bewildered, but I whooped internally with excitement for her.

"That's it, you gained stats! Congratulations, Hana."

"Wow, I actually got them...? I did it, oniichan! I really did it!"

Hana jumped with feverish joy—while still holding the knife. If she hadn't been holding it correctly, I could've witnessed a very different type of fervor.

"Okay, you've breached the first obstacle. The *really* critical part comes next. The skill you gained will determine your future."

"You're right! Um, how do I check my stats display again?"

"You say the command, 'Status open.'"

"Yeah, that's it! Status open!" Her gazed stilled as the screen materialized in front of her. "Cool! It appeared in front of my eyes! Look, oniichan!"

"Yeah, don't worry, don't worry. I'm looking."

I did as she asked and checked her stats display to see what kind of skills she'd obtained. Was Enhanced Strength there? A mana-related skill? Or something to boost a physical ability? What popped up on the display was a string of letters I couldn't believe.

"Is this what I think it is?!" I exclaimed.

AMANE HANA

LEVEL: 2	SP: 100	
HP: 15/15	MP: 5/5	
ATTACK: 3	DEFENSE: 3	SPEED: 3
INTELLIGENCE: 5	RESISTANCE: 3	LUCK: 3

SKILLS: Stock LV 1, Enhanced Strength LV 3, Mana Manipulation LV 3, Mana Boost LV 5

Those last three skills made her plenty capable on their own, but the first one took her skillset from amazing to *astonishing*.

"This is a unique skill...!" I said.

"What?" she asked, perplexed. "Unique skills are skills that no one else in the world has, right? I hear they're incredible."

"With some exceptions." Like Dungeon Teleportation before its true potential awakened. "What matters is the *kinds* of things it can do. Let's check it out."

"Okay!"

Hana and I read the description of Stock's effects together.

STOCK LV 1

CONDITIONS: Directly touching a target copies their skill, so long as it is LV 1 or below.

COPY CAPACITY: Maximum one skill.

COPY DURATION: Maximum ten minutes (note: touching the target again lengthens the effects).

"Wow," I said.

The skill's name was simple enough, but those effects were out of this world. Was this cheating? At this stage, it was limited to copying any skill at LV 1 and only stayed active for ten minutes, but those numbers would undoubtedly increase the more she increased Stock's skill level. Unlike Dungeon Teleportation, this was the type of skill that would expand its capabilities exponentially as she invested SP over time.

Even more amazing was that it copied skills according to *skill* level specifically, rather than their difficulty. Based on this explanation, she could copy advanced skills as easily as novice skills, so long as the skill level qualified. No normal adventurer could obtain advanced skills until level 1,000. Knowing she could adopt them before then was intimidating.

Granted, tons of those advanced skills required buckets of MP, so they might be impossible for her to use. But others didn't require MP at all, or the required MP cost went by percentage instead of points. If she copied the right one, Stock could take her to high places!

In fact, she'd get the best use out of this skill if she joined a strong party. With the right understanding of her party's dynamic, she could borrow their skills and adapt her battle style to add one more knight, tank, or sorcerer to the fight to suit their needs in the moment.

"That's not all," I said to myself.

A wild idea popped into my head. What if Hana copied Dungeon Teleportation and we leveled up together?

There was a hitch, though. She'd need to level up Stock's maximum skill level requirement until it caught up to Dungeon Teleportation's skill level, which was currently LV 16. I didn't plan on slowing down, so maybe she'd never catch up—but I tucked that possibility into my back pocket. After all, that day might one day come.

Beside me, Hana hummed in thought. "Is this a good thing or a bad thing?"

"It's an *amazing* thing. If you announced this power to the world, you'd get instant offers from guilds across Japan."

"Seriously?! That amazing!" She paused for a moment. "I mean, I'm happy it's good, but I don't want the hassle of the guild stuff."

Apparently, Hana wasn't one of the people who wanted to become an adventurer for the fame.

"Don't you want to work as an adventurer?" I asked. "Why *did* you try this out, anyway? In case of accidents?"

"I-it's a secret, okay?! You suck for *prying* into a girl's secrets!"

"Right, got it," I agreed soothingly.

I didn't deserve to be shouted at, but at least angry Hana was adorable.

"If you don't want the attention, you should probably hide Stock when you go report your stats to Katagiri-san," I said. "Only tell people you trust about it. You never know how far that news could reach."

"Is that possible? He might make me show my screen."

"He might—actually, hold on."

I grinned, realizing a way out of this. "I have an idea. Let's test Stock and see if it works."

"What's your idea?"

"A great one."

It wasn't that complicated to guess what I was hinting at, but she was a novice, so I nodded encouragingly and explained my idea: have her copy my Conceal skill and use it on herself. At LV 1, Conceal made for the perfect test *and* the perfect cover. Hana was game immediately.

"Okay, I'll try it... Stock," she said, touching me as she gave the command. Her eyes blinked in surprise. "It worked! The system said, 'Conceal LV 1: Copied.'"

"Good job. Next, you'll need to hide it from your skill list. Here's how you do it."

After I showed her how to use Conceal, she erased it without a hitch. That left one final issue to solve.

"We need to modify Enhanced Strength, Mana Manipulation,

and Mana Boost. Lots of people start with three skills, but the problem is starting at LV 3, 3, and 5. Those are super high for a new adventurer."

"Just make them LV 1, right?"

"That would be normal, yeah."

"Then I'll do it, no problem!"

With a determined nod, Hana overwrote the skill levels to 1. That should cover her secrets.

"Let's head back to everyone else," I said. "And don't tell anyone you used Conceal, or that I have it, got it?"

"Gotcha, but...why *do* you have it? You wouldn't have something like this if you didn't have something to hide."

"I'll tell you later once things settle down."

"Hmm. Fine, I guess."

She dropped the topic faster than a pipin' hot potato, which was unexpected. My moment of relief was interrupted when a sudden air of displacement filled our surroundings. I glanced around, but nothing was there.

"What's the matter, oniichan?"

"It's nothing."

Just my imagination, probably. I put it out of my mind.

We returned to the gathering point with the others. Most of the students had defeated their monsters, since Hana and I spent so much time talking about her stats. A chunk of them were celebrating jubilantly, but most of them were visibly upset. The latter group was unavoidable; 10 percent was 10 percent. In a numbers game, not everyone could win.

Hana showed her Conceal-modified stats display to Katagiri-san, who efficiently confirmed it and congratulated her in a few seconds. I was tense, but it seemed that the process was never going to be very thorough.

After that, everyone who'd defeated a monster left the dungeon, where Katagiri-san addressed the crowd again.

"Those of you who gained stats will participate in dungeon practice two weeks from today. Unlike the monsters this time around, you'll fight monsters with some real bite. We'll show you what to watch out for. After that, you'll receive provisional adventurer qualifications. You may return with an adventurer who has at least one year of experience, but be warned, you will not be permitted to enter the dungeon alone," he explained. "That's it for today. Good work, everyone!"

Everyone dispersed, and Hana and I followed suit.

"Nice job, Hana. Congrats again," I said.

"He he he," she giggled. "Thanks. You should buy me a present to celebrate!"

"Sure, let's drop by the city center. Maybe grab some dinner too."

"Oh? I was half-joking. Aren't we tight on money these days? Are you sure?"

"Don't worry, I've earned plenty recently. Enough to buy you whatever you want."

"Wow! I'll take you up on that!" she said, her hesitation disappearing quickly.

"Great. Also, sounds like you have to attend that dungeon dive training session, but I wouldn't mind doing a test run with you before that, if you want. There's only so much you can learn in a group."

"Really? I'd like that...oh!"

She pulled out her phone and opened a texting app. I turned away so I wouldn't get yelled at for invading a girl's privacy again. I was happy that Hana had a great outcome today and didn't want to kill the mood.

We walked and talked as we traveled down the road. At the time, I didn't sense that someone was watching us from a distance.

The day after Hana gained her stats, I spent the morning at a D-rank dungeon called Minegishi. I wanted to finish up before noon so I could work with Hana in the afternoon, like we promised the day before. We would've planned for the whole day if not for the fact that she *claimed* to have plans in the morning. She was sprawled on the sofa when I left the house earlier, so I couldn't imagine what was so important.

"No need to stick my nose in her business. I'll keep to my dives."

I'd looped Minegishi ever since maxing out Marou, so I imagined I was coming up on the same milestone.

Minegishi's boss was a high goblin and ten lesser goblins. Normally, I'd take each one down with a hit from Nameless, but since there were so many to beat, I messed around with a new move.

"Take this! Nameless Kick!" I shouted.

This was a high-speed technique that I employed while wielding Nameless. I could use it on several opponents at once with relative ease. After I defeated the whole group with a few powerful kicks, the system spoke to me.

"Dungeon Takedown Reward: Level increased by 4!"

"Dungeon Takedown Reward: Level increased by 4!"

"Dungeon Takedown Reward: Level increased by 4!"

"Dungeon Takedown Reward..."

"You have reached this dungeon's maximum number of allotted victories."

"Bonus Reward: Level increased by 10!"

"You will no longer receive rewards for defeating this dungeon."

"Yes! I'm finished."

That took about one hundred victories. A dungeon takedown reward of four levels times one hundred runs plus ten bonus levels for maxing it out equaled...a level boost of 410 levels for me! This made seven dungeons fully 'traveled,' and 5,110 SP gained.

I thought about leveling up Dungeon Teleportation, but one glance at the time made me realize I'd overshot my stay.

"Crap. I lost my head in the dive and forgot the time! I can make it if I hurry, but I gotta run!"

I hurried to Shion Dungeon, our designated meeting point. Shion was the dungeon closest to the station, so the path felt like heading home. I hurried over to the dungeon entrance, where I spotted Hana waiting for me.

"Sorry I'm late, Hana—wait, what?"

Two girls I hadn't expected stood beside her. They faced me as I approached.

"Yui, Rei... Why are you two here?" I asked.

They responded simultaneously.

"I thought it was about time I showed up again," Rei said, calm and expressionless.

"Just felt like it," Yui giggled, posing energetically like an idol.

I glanced between them, bewildered. Their explanations were not exactly explanatory.

Hana puffed her cheeks at me. "Jeez, Oniichan. Way to cut it close!"

"Sorry, okay? So *why* are they here, exactly?"

"I invited Yui-senpai yesterday. She always asks about you when we talk, so I figured I'd bring her!"

"Hana-chan, what are you talking about?! Rin-senpai, don't believe her!" Yui cried.

"Okay, I won't," I replied simply.

"W-well, you could believe her a little bit," she amended while poking her two index fingers together.

Make a decision, Yui, I thought as I turned to my second surprise visitor. "What about you, Rei? I didn't know you knew Hana."

"Yui told me about her plans today. I came along since she told me you'd be here."

"Um, right..."

The blunt way she said it shut me right up. She came specifically to see me? Well, gee. When did I become Mr. Popular? Not that I was opposed!

"As promised, here's the money I owe you," she said, handing me an envelope full of cash. "I worked hard this last week to save it."

No popular phase for me, I thought, deflating. Just good old-fashioned business.

Seeing the exchange, Hana and Yui's eyes widened.

"O-oniichan! You're taking money from younger girls?!"

"You're terrible, Rin-senpai! I'm really disappointed in you!"

"Wait, wait, wait! Why?! Don't assume things!" I said, desperate to stop the freight trains of their imagination from barreling off a cliff. "Rei, say something to them!"

"Okay." She nodded and pressed her hands to her chest. "Rin is very special to me. He's the reason I'm here. I'm giving him money because I want to, not because I have to, so don't worry about me. In fact, I worry this isn't enough—"

"Hold up, Rei. You're skipping the important parts and making this worse!"

I know I asked her to keep Dungeon Teleportation a secret, so she had to gloss over *some* details, but the way she put it made it sound like I'd brainwashed her!

"Oniichan?"

"Rin-senpai!"

Both of them turned on me with a furious fire in their eyes.

It took a solid five minutes to convince them to lower their hackles and unravel the misunderstanding.

Once that *ordeal* was out of the way, the four of us entered Shion and headed down to the lower floors. Hana was walking in the center with big enthusiastic steps as she spoke.

"So, when you encountered Rei-san inside a dungeon, you used an expensive item to save her? You should've started with that!"

"I explained it like, ten times already."

"For what it counts, I believed you from the start, Rin-senpai!" Yui said indignantly.

"Says you!" I tugged on Yui's cheek gently.

"Owwwwooo, noooo," she whined, pretending to be gravely wounded.

"Grr. Ha ha ha, very funny."

While I was teasing Yui, Rei maneuvered herself to my side and tilted her head toward me. "Sorry, Rin. I should've given you the money somewhere more appropriate."

"Oh, that's no big deal. I'm just surprised you managed to earn so much in such a short amount of time."

"I didn't beat any dungeons this last week. I focused on valuable monsters I could hunt on my own," she replied. "I also used the time to reevaluate myself."

I paused, unsure how to respond to that final part. "I see."

Rei didn't belong to any parties or guilds anymore. This *was* an excellent chance for her to reassess her values and think about the kind of adventurer she wanted to become.

"Good luck, Rei," I told her. Genuinely, I wanted her to succeed.

"Thanks, Rin."

I noticed Yui squinting at us as if we were two cells under a microscope. "I've been wondering, how close *are* you two? You're younger, Rei, but you don't use honorifics or anything. Wait! Are you two, like, a lovey-dovey couple already?!"

"Why am I getting déjà vu?" I retorted, but thinking on it, Yui wasn't completely off base. Rei and I definitely had a vibe going as soon as we met. I hadn't thought deeply about it, but I definitely didn't mind the dynamic.

That wasn't romantic, though. "A lack of honorifics doesn't make us a couple. You can drop mine if you want to, Yui."

"Um, that's a bit...*much* for me. People would get the wrong idea, you know..."

Yui sure grew fidgety real fast for someone who liked to point fingers at everyone but herself. That reminded me of the time Hana told me Yui tended to jump to conclusions. Then again, watching her squirm *was* kind of fun...

Minutes passed as we expanded the conversation to other topics: school, dungeons, whatever. Eventually, we reached our destination, which would serve as the central point of our activities for the day.

The goal was to teach Hana how adventurers operated. At the same time, I wanted her to practice her Stock skill as much as possible. That being said...

"Hana, Yui and Rei will learn your skill. Are you comfortable with that?" I asked—to the air! She'd wandered off.

I called out, "Hey! Hana!"

Hana bounded back to me. "What's up, oniichan?"

"My main goal today is getting you some field experience as an adventurer and possibly testing out Stock. But with Yui and Rei here, I wanted to ask how you feel about doing that."

"Fine by me! I don't mind if they know."

"Are you sure? I understand that you trust Yui, but you've never met Rei before."

"If you're leaving the decision to me, then that means you trust Rei-senpai not to say anything. *Ergo*, it'll be fine," she finished confidently.

"Huh. Makes sense."

That was how much Hana trusted *me*. As much as that warmed my heart, a corner of my mind stayed cool and analytical. I still hadn't told Hana about Dungeon Teleportation's true worth. Not because I didn't trust her, but because I needed to find the right time for it.

Dungeon Teleportation was unusual, even among unique skills. As useless as it was in battle compared to other skills, it was *many* times more effective than normal methods of leveling up. Having our lives targeted because of my unique skill's nature wasn't outside the realm of possibility. It didn't feel great to admit it, but I was better off keeping it to myself for now. Without any sponsors or others supporting me, I just couldn't let my skill's existence spread around.

"Support, huh?" I mumbled. On the other hand, if I had support, I *could* go public with my ability and secure enough backing to protect Hana. Maybe a national or powerful local guild. It would have to be a guild with some of the world's top rankers among them to really impact my safety. To join a group like that, I needed to build more strength.

Either way, I would wait a little longer before I told Hana about my power.

With her input in mind, I decided we'd focus on testing Stock first. I gave Yui and Rei a quick run-down about how Yui's skill worked. They both stared at me with astonishment.

"That's an amazing skill." Rei folded her arms and nodded authoritatively. "I'd expect nothing less from Rin's little sister."

Who was she to make that comment, a Rin expert?

Yui had an even bigger reaction. "A unique skill? *Wooooow*, that's so awesome, Hana-chan! Rei-chan has one too, which means half of us here are unique skill holders!"

She turned to me. "What do we do, Rin-senpai? You and I don't have unique skills. It's almost like we're in their shadows!"

"Huh?" I replied.

"'Huh,' what?" she asked, blinking in confusion.

Oops. I hadn't told her about my skill, had I?

Helpfully, Hana threw me a lifeline. "Yui-senpai, oniichan *does* have a unique skill."

"What?! Rin-senpai, you never told me! You traitor!"

"It's a weak and useless skill in battle, though," Hana continued.

"I trusted you, Rin-senpai! Start acting like you care about me—"

I pulled Yui's cheeks gently while she whined.

"Rei-senpai, you have a unique skill too?" Hana asked over Yui's complaints.

"Yeah. It's called Magic Sword." Rei swept up a whirl of mana in front of her and uttered a command. "Quartet."

From the cloud of magic, four elemental swords manifested: flame, ice, wind, and lightning. As they floated and revolved around her body, she explained further. "I imagine the sword I want to create and manifest them, just like this. I've summoned swords of wind that can sever enemies from a distance, swords that explode upon contact, and other various types. The more complicated the features are, the more MP they cost."

"That's incredible...!" Hana said.

"Yeah. They're pretty too!" Yui added.

Having teamed up with Rei myself, I agreed with their praise wholeheartedly. I'd witnessed her versatile flame and wind swords in action. Even seeing her four elemental swords at rest around her was a spectacle, in and of itself. On that note, why did they come out in the shape of swords? Probably something inherent to the magic itself. Whatever the reason, it was a powerful unique skill, useful enough to rival Hana's Stock skill.

Her demonstration finished, Rei dispelled her magic swords and turned to me. "So, Rin. What do we do now?"

"I wanted to test out Stock, so..."

The fastest way to see what Stock could do was to have Hana copy an attack-based skill, but she couldn't copy anything above LV 1. Conceal was the only skill I knew that low-level, but I didn't need to scrape up another one. We had two other adventurers for her to borrow from. I doubt Hana invited them for that reason, but hey, Luck was a stat too. My little sister was a genius, whether she knew it or not!

While I quietly burst with brotherly pride, I turned to Yui and Rei. "Would you two let Hana copy one of your attack-based skills at LV 1?"

They glanced at each other and smirked as if communicating some kind of challenge, then looked to me.

"Sorry, I only have skills at LV 2 or above," Rei said.

"And I only have one attack-based skill!" Yui added.

Okay, well, show over! Everybody pack it in!

Not one of us had an attack-based skill Hana could copy. I was stumped—but then Yui clapped and rubbed her hands together like a smug racoon. "I know!" she said. "I'd been meaning to obtain a new one, so now's a better time than any. Give me Novice Magic LV1!"

She nodded, indicating the system voice said she'd obtained Novice Magic.

"Yui, you didn't need to waste SP on a new skill just for us," I said.

"Actually, my senior guildmates told me I should have at least one attack-based skill to protect myself. It's perfect timing!"

"Really? At your level SP is a valuable commodity, remember? Are you sure you're okay with the way you used it?"

"Don't you worry about my SP. I broke level 150 the other day!"

My eyes widened. "Weren't you level 80 when we first met? I'm impressed you improved that much in such a short time."

"*He he he.* My guild is the real superstar. The guild members know all kinds of ways to level up effectively! They're teaching me *aaaaaall* their secrets."

True, Yui was a member of the Yoizuki Guild. As one of the nation's leading guilds, they could provide her a lot of benefits.

Yui spoke again suddenly. "That reminds me! Listen to *this,* Rin-senpai. There's this *suuuper* cool senpai at my guild. He's two years older than me, gentle, polite, talented, and all of our guild members respect him. He's teaching me *sooo* many things! Does that, say, spark any feelings in you?"

"Uh, I'm glad for you?"

She grumbled at my answer. "You know what, Rin-senpai? I don't care anymore! Hmph!"

It seemed like our communication had melted down somewhere yet again, but I couldn't tell where. Oh, well. I would just address what she said and not try to read into it.

"Seriously, obtaining Novice Magic was a huge help. Thank you," I said.

"W-well, it's nice to be thanked. I kindly accept your gratitude!" she answered, her expression wavering as if she was trying to hide a grin. With her help, we could finally put Stock to the test.

"Okay, I'm gonna borrow your skill, Yui-senpai," Hana said.

"Go for it!"

"Stock!" Hana commanded. A moment of silence, then, "Yep, that copied it!"

With her copied skill ready, we headed for a battle with a monster.

"Hana and Yui, I want to see the differences when you cast the same magic. Yui, will you start?" I asked.

"Leave it to me!"

While we talked, a lesser wolf crossed our path. At level five, it was a scrawny one.

"Yui," I prompted.

"I know... Fireball!"

An orb of flame shot from Yui's hand and struck the lesser wolf head on. The wolf yelped and went down from that single attack.

"You next, Hana," I said. "Are you ready?"

"Right, um, yeah! I've got this!" she replied. Contrary to her claim, she was clearly nervous to wield magic for the first time, but I'd taught her how to use it. I was sure she'd be fine.

Another lesser wolf crossed our path. Hana stepped in front of the rest of us and shouted, "Fireball!"

The ball of fire that left Hana's hand was smaller than Yui's. The wolf wavered on impact, but it swiftly righted itself and dashed toward Hana—

And yelped as my kick sent it flying. In a second, it thudded to a stop and expired. I turned back to everyone to discuss the result of the test.

"It doesn't look like Stock can replicate the strength of the lender's magic," I said.

Magic strength was calculated from skill level and Intelligence. Hana's low level dictated her low Intelligence when compared to Yui's, which meant she couldn't output the same power Yui could.

"Even a unique skill can't replicate a high-level adventurer's exact power," I said.

"So does that mean my skill is weak?" Hana asked.

"Far from it. Think of it the other way around: if you have higher stats, the skill you copy could have *greater* output than the host. All skills have fixed damage outputs according to skill level. It just depends on how you wield them."

"Okay...in that case, I've gotta work even harder to get strong!"

"Exactly."

With our understanding of Stock improved, we spent the rest of the time teaching her the ins and outs of adventuring. Once I explained my fair share, I split off to take a break and watch Hana, Yui, and Rei fight monsters together.

That was when something crazy came to my mind.

"Rei can handle close combat and mid-range battles, Yui specializes in ranged abilities, and Hana can match either of them to suit their needs. Together, they're surprisingly balanced," I mused to myself. "With someone who specializes in forward defense...a tank, maybe, they'd form a strong party."

That was just an idle daydream though. It wasn't rooted in reality. Their levels were far apart, and Yui already belonged to a guild. My ruminations were nothing more than fantasy. At best, they might end up at the same guild at similar levels one day.

"Either way, that's nothing I can do anything about *now*."

We continued through the dungeon for another hour or so. I'd told Hana everything I wanted her to know, so she went off to spend some low-level adventuring time with Rei and Yui. Overall, it was a pretty productive day.

The next day, I returned to the dungeon diving grind. It would take another week before I maxed out the tenth and final dungeon needed to complete the Dungeon Traveler title.

I was on the last floor of Niimi—a C-rank dungeon—when the system dinged.

"You have reached this dungeon's maximum number of allotted victories."

"Bonus Reward: Level increased by 25!"

"You will no longer receive rewards for defeating this dungeon."

"It's *over!*" I exclaimed. At last, I'd maxed out my tenth dungeon and completed my Dungeon Traveler title. Who could blame me for shouting with joy?

"Oops, I better check the title to make sure."

I pulled up the stats display.

DUNGEON TRAVELER (10/10)
A title granted to someone who has traversed a dungeon in its entirety.

> By traveling a dungeon a specific number of times, this person
> gains special benefits.

The bullet point about benefits—now *that* was new and intriguing. Would it activate passive effects, or would it give me some kind of skill? Maybe I should've held my horses on the celebration. I didn't know anything yet.

"What will I get?" I wondered aloud. "Dungeon Teleportation allowed me to level up at speeds unheard of for anyone in just two months of adventuring. I expect this benefit to be something significant too..."

At least, that was what I hoped. The benefit that *actually* showed up on the display was quite a swerve from what I pictured.

"The title holder's ten completed dungeons have been confirmed."

"The title holder has gained the right to challenge an extra dungeon: The Remote Magic Tower."

I tilted my head like a dog trying to understand human speech. "The *what* now?"

I couldn't make sense of what the system told me. Did it just say, 'the right to challenge the Remote Magic Tower?' Not that the system picked up on my confusion, but it *did* continue.

"The title holder's current status has been input."

"The title holder cannot level up until they have challenged the Remote Magic Tower."

"Adjusting the Remote Magic Tower to suit the title holder's stats."

"*ERROR. The Remote Magic Tower does not exist. The title holder has been confirmed as the tower's first challenger.*"

"*Now spawning the Remote Magic Tower.*"

In the next moment, the whole dungeon—no, the *whole world*—began to tremble.

"*What the hell's going on?!*" I shouted.

Without a working cell phone or telepathy, I couldn't confirm what was happening during the literal earthquake, so I braced myself and endured it. It went on for several minutes. When it finally stopped, the system spoke again.

"*The Remote Magic Tower has been spawned.*"

"*It will await the title holder's challenge.*"

After that, the system said nothing else. Like a parting gift, a piece of paper fluttered down in front of me.

"What on earth?" I grumbled. Appraisal provided the insight I needed.

REMOTE MAGIC TOWER CHALLENGER'S TICKET
TITLE HOLDER: Amane Rin
A ticket given to those who explore ten dungeons to completion.
Tearing this ticket apart within the vicinity of the Remote Magic
    Tower permits one challenge attempt.

"Honestly, I can't keep up with everything the system's throwing at me. Now it's telling me to use this to enter the 'Remote Magic Tower?'"

Frankly, I wasn't that interested in exploring a weird new

tower, but the problem was what the system said: until I challenged the Remote Magic Tower, I was 'barred from leveling up
any further.' I had no choice *but* to challenge it.

"What *is* the Remote Magic Tower?" I wondered. "I've never
heard the name, and I don't have any means to locate it—oh!"
Light gathered around me. "Right, the teleportation spell is
activating."

That was a longer wait than usual for it to activate. Something
to do with the earthquake? At least it still worked. Once the spell
plopped me in the Return Zone, I exited to the surface.

Something in the distance drew my attention immediately.

"Are you serious...?"

The sight before me rendered me speechless. Not just me—
the people around me were looking in the same direction with
wide eyes. As if boldly grasping for the heavens, a massive tower
now loomed immensely in the distance, reaching brazenly into
the sky. Until today—no, until *a few minutes ago*—that tower
didn't exist. If the system was correct, I was the only person on
the planet who knew what it was.

"That must be the Remote Magic Tower...the dungeon I *have*
to challenge."

Back then, I hardly knew the meaning of the word. It wasn't
until I experienced the Remote Magic Tower that I understood
what challenging a dungeon truly meant.

AMANE RIN

LEVEL: 6,604   **SP:** 3,010

TITLES: Dungeon Traveler (10/10), Nameless Swordsman,
    Endbringer (ERROR)

HP: 52,100/52,100   **MP:** 13,940/13,940

ATTACK: 12,630   **DEFENSE:** 10,580   **SPEED:** 13,430

INTELLIGENCE: 9,970   **RESISTANCE:** 10,010   **LUCK:** 9,420

SKILLS: Dungeon Teleportation LV 18, Enhanced Strength LV MAX,
    Herculean Strength LV MAX, Superhuman Strength LV 6,
    High-speed Movement LV MAX, Gale Wind LV 6, Mana Boost LV 2,
    Mana Recovery LV 2, Enemy Detection LV 4, Evasion LV 4,
    Status Condition Resistance LV 4, Appraisal, Item Box LV 5,
    Conceal LV 1

DUNGEON TELEPORTATION LV 18

REQUIRED MP: 2 MP × Distance (meters)

CONDITIONS: Teleportation can only occur in dungeons that have
    already been visited.

TELEPORTATION DISTANCE: Maximum 400 meters.

ACTIVATION TIME: 0.8 seconds × distance (meters)

SCOPE: User and user's belongings.

SWORD OF THE NAMELESS KNIGHT

A sword used by the Nameless Knight.

RECOMMENDED EQUIP LEVEL: 6,000

ATTACK +6,000

When an enemy (human or monster) is of a higher level than the wielder, all parameters except HP and MP increase by 56% each.

CHAPTER 3

THE REMOTE MAGIC TOWER

THE NIGHT THAT the extra dungeon—the Remote Magic Tower—spawned, the story was *buzzing* on the talk shows. Hana and I watched the reporter on TV discuss it.

"As you can see, a building that resembles a dungeon of some sort has materialized, but it features many characteristics unusual for dungeons. Its sudden appearance aside, this one takes the shape of a giant tower. The tower extends higher than the clouds, but we have no way of confirming its internal construction or mechanisms. Due to the absence of a Gate to enter it, further investigation seems impossible. We're left with many questions..."

"An above-ground dungeon? That *is* strange," Hana said.

I nodded. "Yeah. It is."

Only I knew it was called the Remote Magic Tower, but even I didn't know why it formed above ground. Would I learn the reason once I stepped inside? Whatever I speculated, I had to face it. I was fit and ready, so I had no excuse not to go the next day.

Nevertheless, a few concerns lingered on my mind. First, I would become the dungeon's first challenger, which meant I'd enter without any information. I needed to prepare for every scenario conceivable. I didn't know if I could defeat the dungeon within the same day, so I had to pack food too. As I often had, I gave a moment of appreciation to my Item Box.

The last thing I had to do before leaving was give a heads-up to Hana.

"Hana," I said, "I'm sorry, but I need to travel tomorrow, and I'm not sure if I'll make it back home for a few days."

"Where are you going?"

"It's...a secret."

"Wait! Did you get a girlfriend?!"

"*No*. When have I ever mentioned someone like that?"

"Sorry, oniichan..." For some reason, her apology was heavy with sincerity. Ha, I wasn't even angry!

After a pause, Hana spoke again. "How long is 'a few days'? I have that second dungeon trip, you know. Will you make it back for that?"

"Shoot. I forgot about that."

Hana was required to attend practice to obtain her official adventurer qualifications. Escorts were allowed to attend those too, so I wanted to be there for her if possible.

"I can't say yes for certain, but I'll do everything I can to be back in time, I promise," I promised.

"Okay. You already taught me so much, I think I'll be okay without an escort."

"Hey, no underestimating dungeons while I'm gone, you hear?"

"I know, I know."

After our talk, I headed to my room to prepare for an early day and get some rest.

What awaited me at the Remote Magic Tower?

Half hopeful and half anxious, I fell asleep.

On the way to the Remote Magic Tower the next day, I dropped by a general store for adventurers. I would make good use of the 50 million yen I'd saved up to buy all the necessities: health recovery potions, mana recovery potions, giant Exploding Stones, and a brand-new short sword. Those items should bail me out of any dicey situations I might face.

Once I paid, I headed for the Remote Magic Tower on foot. It was located about an hour from our home. The giant building towered over a clearing outside of town, full of nature, with no human residences nearby. As I approached, I saw scores of Dungeon Association staff members surrounding the tower's base.

"Of course they'd investigate something that popped up out of nowhere. Guess I have to use Conceal."

Careful not to catch their attention, I used Conceal on myself and sneaked toward the tower's base. I feared someone among them might have a high-level Enemy Detection skill, but it seemed I didn't need to worry: nobody noticed me.

"This should be close enough," I told myself.

I withdrew the Remote Magic Tower Challenger's Ticket from my Item Box.

This ticket was for one shot at the tower. I didn't hesitate—
I ripped the ticket.

The white glow of mana enveloped my body.

"Okay, Remote Magic Tower. Show me what I worked so hard
to unlock," I said.

The teleportation spell activated and whisked me away.

The spell dropped me inside the Remote Magic Tower, and
the bizarre sight before me made my eyes widen.

"What *is* all this?" I whispered.

A verdant, thick field of rich green grass stretched in every
direction. The tower's outer circumference suggested I should see
the end of it, but no matter which direction I turned, I didn't see
walls anywhere. The greatest shock came from looking *up*, where
a blue sky, as clear and cloudless as a hot summer day, greeted me.

If I told anyone what existed inside this tower, would they
believe me?

"The size of this place, let alone a *sky inside a tower*, doesn't
make physical or logical sense. Is magic responsible for expanding
it? I've never heard of a dungeon or spell like this, but that's what
you get from a *magic* tower, I guess. The first of its kind for sure..."

I could hypothesize a few possibilities for how the tower
worked, but I wasn't a scientist or a sorcerer, so there was no way
to tell for sure. Mulling over it to myself more was a waste of time.
Instead, I considered my actionable tasks.

"This doesn't seem like a normal dungeon, but does Dungeon Teleportation work in here? Better check... Dungeon Teleportation!"

The command moved me one meter from where I'd been standing. Cool. If my skill could activate, even if this was the weirdest, most magic tower in the world, it still qualified as a dungeon. The real issue was what I would do next.

"I figure I should aim to ascend the levels, since this is a tower and all...but there aren't any stairs. Not to mention there's *sky* above me. This is getting complex already."

For the time being, it was best to explore the area.

The second I thought that, the system cut me off.

"Title holder Amane Rin has entered the Remote Magic Tower."

"The Remote Magic Tower consists of ten levels."

"Each level comes with a quest. Complete the quest and proceed to the next level."

"Level one quest: Exterminate the magic wolves. You must defeat all monsters on this level."

The messages ended there. That was the extent of what it planned to tell me.

"One quest per level, huh? This is just like a video game," I groaned. "Oh, well. The only way up is through!"

If I had to exterminate every monster on this level to proceed, then I simply would. I used Enemy Detection to survey the area and found monsters immediately.

"Five monsters a short distance away. They're moving at a fast pa—wait. Are they headed *right at me*?"

It didn't take long to confirm I was right. Barely ten seconds later, the five monsters leapt into view. Were those—

"Fire wolves?"

I'd fought packs of those in Marou the other day. The five-strong horde came at me in a flash of red fur.

"I get it now. This'll be like fighting in Marou. Just gotta defeat them, right?"

I withdrew Nameless from my Item Box and used Appraisal on the nearest fire wolf, but the results blindsided me.

FIRE WOLF

LEVEL: 4,000

A wolf-type monster with fire-resistant fur. It moves agilely and breathes fire.

"Level *4,000*?!" I exclaimed. That number was *way* over what I imagined. The ones that spawned in Marou hovered around level 1,000. Compared to that, these ones were *beasts*. Their small bodies hid power well above that of the Rainbow King Wolf. They might be lower level than I was, but I couldn't let my guard down.

"Here goes nothing!"

Without hesitation, I dashed toward them and launched an attack. I was equipped with the Ring of Marou (True), but the fire wolves' magic attacks were still nasty. I had to take them down before they could try anything tricky with me!

"Take *this*!" I shouted.

The wolf snarled in surprise. Before it could summon a burst of fire, my rapid attack struck true and severed its head from its body. Four wolves remained. I had a ways to go before I could relax.

The rest of them snapped and whined as I followed through with attacks in quick succession. Searing fire flew through the air. I evaded, feeling the scorching heat of their magic as it passed close by, and used the momentum of dodging to slash them with my sword.

"Number two!" I cried, as the head dropped off the second one. I whirled on the third one in the same breath. One of the fire wolves launched its fireball at me, but I ducked out of the way and the flames scorched the other wolves. At the same time, I strained to follow through with another attack, surprising them. Using the window of opportunity, I slashed frantically.

"Third one!"

"Fourth one!"

"You're last, number five!"

In ten seconds flat, the last three collapsed. Somehow, I'd ended the fight without a scratch, but *dang*, was it a struggle.

The downed wolves suddenly vanished. What a shame. This dungeon didn't even leave rewards for harvesting.

"At least all five went down. I managed fine, but a pack of ten or more would be a handful. Not to mention the different species of wolves. This could get seriously rough in the long run..."

And I was 100 percent certain there would be a long run. Like I said earlier, there was no way up but through.

"How many monsters exist on this level anyway? One

hundred? Two hundred? I can manage that, but more than five hundred could get chancy."

The more there were, the more HP and MP the fights would cost me. Soloing had its downsides—weak monsters chipped away at my stamina more than they would with a party to carry some of the burden. A group could also defeat powerful monsters that much easier.

"Argh, but I don't have time to complain. I've got to keep my head up, complete this quest, and make it to the next level!"

That was when it happened.

Vibrations strong enough to shake my legs shuddered through the ground.

"What's going on?" I wondered aloud. I whipped my head around to find the source of the vibrations—and unfortunately, I found it.

"Hold up." I squinted. "What *is* that?"

A massive black shadow advanced across the field toward me. Rather, it wasn't a single shadow. It was so many monsters gathered together that they appeared to form a single unit from afar.

This quest wasn't a question of killing one hundred or two hundred monsters.

A display popped up in front of me. Reading it made me curse the world.

LEVEL ONE QUEST: MAGIC WOLF EXTERMINATION
Defeat all monsters on level one.
MONSTERS DEFEATED: 5/5,000

"Um...can I go home now?" I pleaded to the bright blue sky.

Yeah, at this point, I think I was allowed to complain.

That was the beginning of hell on earth.

"Gained XP: Level increased by 1!"

"Gained XP: Level increased by 1!"

"Gained XP: Level increased by 1!"

How much time had passed since I started fighting this horde of magic wolves? Was I always fighting them? Was my life before magic wolves just a dream?

I barely had time to consider the question. I poured every bit of mental and physical energy into staving off the enormous horde of wolves.

"Haaaaa!" I roared. Like the silver flash of a barracuda, I thrust my short sword forward. The blade dug deeply into a poison wolf's throat.

> **SPEED SWORD**
> A short sword made with a Blacksmith skill.
> **RECOMMENDED EQUIP LEVEL:** 4,000
> **ATTACK** +3,000
> **SPEED** +1,500

This was the short sword I purchased before I came to the Remote Magic Tower. Unlike the other weapons I'd equipped, someone with a Blacksmith skill made it—and it was a good thing I bought it, because I needed it in a scenario like this one. Using Nameless against monsters of a lower level rendered its abilities inactive, so I wanted something light that wouldn't slow me down. A short sword kept my speed parameters up and enabled me to move with maximum agility. It dinged me with a slight Attack decrease, but it didn't stop me from making one-hit kills, so I coped.

I utilized the expansiveness of the battleground and dashed around, evading every wolf that tried to take a bite out of me. Water wolves and earth wolves launched their magic attacks relentlessly. I did my best to dodge the attacks as they sailed through the air, but I was late sometimes. They grazed me.

The Ring of Marou (True) lessened the damage I took, but the attacks still chipped at my HP. I couldn't take hits forever. If I weakened, my chances would only go downhill. My HP was already down by 20 percent.

"I have no choice—Gale Wind!" I commanded.

Gale Wind: +60% to speed (costs 10 MP per second)

I'd avoided MP-draining skills because I thought this battle would be a long one, but a frantic battlefield like this required conviction. I had to go hard *and* fast to clear the quest and survive!

"I *will* finish this!" I vowed, continuing my assault on the magic wolves. I screamed a war cry.

"Yaaaaah!"

"Gained XP: Level increased by 1!"

"Gained XP: Level increased by 1!"

"Gained XP: Level increased by 1!"

Time passed, and many more wolves fell to my blade. My hands grew numb, and fatigue nipped at my heels. I'd defeated most of the wolves from the first wave and thought I'd earned a break, but the tower disagreed with me. Two threatening howls rose across the grass. I whirled in their direction.

"Are those what I *think* they are?!" I exclaimed in exasperation.

RAINBOW KING WOLF
LEVEL: 7,000
A wolf-like monster with multicolored fur in a lustrous range of nine shades. It possesses agility unprecedented for its large frame and attacks with a variety of magic.

The two rainbow king wolves were a head taller than the other wolves, and they were *powerful* beasts. These after the nearly one thousand magic wolves already beaten? Man, this quest was merciless!

"Actually, time for a break!" I shouted. Compared to the other magic wolves, two higher-level ones were easier! I swapped my weapon to Nameless and charged. Thanks to their slightly higher level than me, Nameless's abilities kicked into effect. That made them a piece of cake to beat compared to a horde of a hundred lower-level magic wolves. Time for a bonus round!

"Thanks for being my punching bags!" I yelled.

I threw my frustration into Nameless and chopped at them countless times with a wild, sloppy style. My technique was a mess, but I successfully defeated the rainbow king wolves regardless. First wave down.

"Gained XP: Level increased by 10!"

"Gained XP: Level increased by 9!"

LEVEL ONE QUEST: MAGIC WOLF EXTERMINATION
Defeat all monsters on level one.
MONSTERS DEFEATED: 1032/5,000

"Whew...that's one-fifth of the horde," I sighed.

As I drank a health recovery potion and a mana recovery potion, I analyzed the situation. I'd been fighting for over an hour and only defeated a fraction of the monsters I needed to complete the quest. I could feel it wearing on me not only mentally but physically. Potions recovered my HP and MP, but they couldn't cure fatigue. The battle was only going to get more strenuous as the next waves hit.

"I should increase my skill levels," I decided.

I opened my stats display and found the forty levels and 3,610 SP I'd accumulated during the fight. I decided to dump all of it into one skill—Mana Boost, which elevated it from LV 2 to LV 5.

Mana Boost LV 5: +50% to MP

"Good. This should make Gale Wind last longer. The battle was much easier while using it, so I want to extend its duration for the rest."

I was up against an army. Any misstep would find me trampled by a wolf stampede. From start to finish, this fight required every play in my book.

Another tremor ran through the ground, bigger than before. I snapped into stance with my Speed Sword.

"All right." I steadied myself. "Here we go."

I sped forward and dived into the turbulent sea of magic wolves.

The battle made time truly seem like a figment of my imagination. Three thousand magic wolves died by my hand, but I lost count after that. Waves three and four rushed me in quick succession, too fast to keep track of the numbers. Over the incessant howling and bloodshed, I couldn't hear the system update either.

Reflex propelled me around each magic attack and kept me swinging and beheading wolves. It was all that sustained me. My mind whittled down to instinct and left no room for thought—except one, deep inside. There, in the one corner of my mind not occupied with exterminating wolves, I had a sobering realization.

Most adventurers, like most people, were careful: they challenged dungeons appropriate for their ability level and made informed preparations beforehand. That was the worldwide standard. Naturally, I was no exception. But some people—some A-rank adventurers—*were* exceptional and fought outside of that cushion of safety. Even more so for S-rank adventurers. Like the ancient explorers who first navigated unknown lands, they traversed unexplored, high-difficulty dungeons daily. To them, following the norm was abnormal. They sought stronger opponents as if they were called to it.

Now, I understood why.

That was what it meant to conquer dungeons—to dance on the knife's edge, where one wrong move would result in death. To know that, but to press on anyway, and to *win*. Only those who overcame that challenge received a truly worthwhile reward.

That was what I was doing now, like the top-class adventurers that came before me.

With every aching muscle in my body, I wanted to catch up to them.

No, that wasn't enough.

I needed to *surpass* them to stand on top of the world. If they had already fought through the pits of hell, I needed to dig even deeper than that. I wasn't there yet, was only taking the first step on a long journey, and I knew that. But I would get there someday.

"I won't stop here!!!" I cried as my sword flew through the air. It didn't matter how tired I got. If a tall obstacle stood in front of me, I would find a way to climb it. I would never quit.

"Gained XP: Level increased by 1!"

"Gained XP: Level increased by 8!"

"Gained XP: Level increased by 1!"

I used my short sword against lower-level enemies and Nameless against higher-level enemies. When I lost power to fatigue, that only forced my movements to become more efficient.

Five hours after the battle began, the moment finally arrived.

"Raaaaaaah!" I bellowed. In less than ten seconds, I chopped the heads from ten level-7,000 rainbow king wolves. As the momentum from Nameless propelled me, I whirled around and searched for my next target.

"Wait...where's the next one?" I panted.

There *were* no next ones.

Without a target, I cautiously lowered Nameless. The system then spoke.

"Level One Quest: Magic Wolf Extermination is complete."

"Level one takedown reward: Level increased by 50!"

> **LEVEL ONE QUEST: MAGIC WOLF EXTERMINATION**
> Defeat all monsters on level one.
> **MONSTERS DEFEATED:** 5,000/5,000

In a daze, I glanced around the endless field.

"...It's really over?"

It was. It really, truly was.

I had beaten level one of the Remote Magic Tower.

> **LEVEL:** 6,604 → 6,900
> Total levels gained within the Remote Magic Tower: 296 (level one complete)

The system's confirmation that I completed the quest filled me with excitement.

"It's over!" I cheered, flopping on my back amidst the abundant grass.

Glad as I was, I was *exhausted*. The transition from battle brain back to normal brain left me feeling as hollow as a dried cicada shell.

"I'm so tired... How did I fight like this? Shout out to me, honestly."

Just when I was complimenting myself, the system spoke again.

"You may now attempt level two."

"You have two options: attempt the next challenge within the next twenty-four hours or retire. Please choose one."

"In the event that you choose to retire, you will not be allowed to challenge the Remote Magic Tower again."

Well, those were my options.

If I doubted my chances moving forward, I could bail—or I could take the next twenty-four hours to rest and refuel.

"Time to make a decision. I really have to consider a few things," I told myself.

First, whether I could reenter the Remote Magic Tower with Dungeon Teleportation. If it was possible, withdrawing for a time could be a sensible move. After all, it seemed I could level up again since I'd entered the tower. Maybe I could return to other dungeons, grind, and return strong enough for an easy victory. The idea was tempting.

"But this place isn't like other dungeons. Who knows if Dungeon Teleportation will let me back in, and there's no guarantee the quests will reactivate."

If the system was trustworthy, I needed to complete each quest to proceed to the next level of the tower. The odds of excellent take-down rewards for a demanding dungeon like this one were high. I wanted a shot at them. If I left, I risked losing out on them forever.

"That leaves me with one answer," I concluded. "I'm proceeding to the next level!"

Although, that didn't mean I would head to level two right away. I wanted time to recover my HP, MP, and overall stamina. I'd make use of the entire twenty-four-hour rest period to return to my best!

"At a minimum, I badly need nutrients, stat," I said.

I dragged my body upright and withdrew some of the food and water I'd stored inside Item Box. I didn't have much of an appetite, but I forced myself to eat. Afterward, I pulled a sleeping bag from Item Box.

"Glad I prepared for roughing it. This'll make it tough to react to a sudden attack, but based on the quest, I doubt there are any monsters left on this level..."

I slipped into the sleeping bag and promptly dozed off—just kidding! I tried to, but it wasn't that simple.

"It's so bright out!" I shouted at the vast space. Remember, I was in an unnatural grass field under a sunny summer sky. How could I possibly sleep? Frustrated, I voiced that toward the system. "Oi, system! Can't you do something about this stupid daylight?!"

I was only venting, so I expected neither a response nor a reaction. Imagine my shock when the sky switched from daylight to nighttime with the speed of a light switch.

"Huh?!" I gaped.

"Seriously, did it...did it listen to me? Could the system actually be *nice*?"

I gasped in horror, realizing that I'd nearly softened my heart toward the merciless system that governed this whole dungeon mess.

"C'mon, me. Get a grip! The system *just* put me on the brink of death, like it loves to do. Showing a little kindness after that is the classic cycle of abuse. I nearly fell for it..."

I'd evaded manipulation by a hair's breadth. The system was garbage. I repeated it aloud so I wouldn't forget.

"The system is *garbage!*"

The sky brightened with daylight.

"I was lying! I'm sorry!" I shouted frantically.

The sky returned to nighttime.

"What the heck?" I wondered aloud. "It's like the system has feelings... Ugh, whatever. I'll just sleep."

I was beyond over this day, so I curled up in my sleeping bag and shut my eyes. After some time to calm down and drift off, I slept soundly for ten hours.

Once I woke from my deep sleep, I tested out my condition with some light stretching.

"Hmm, not bad. Most of my HP and MP are back. Time to

head to the next level." I wanted to enter the second level immediately, but there was an obvious issue.

How do I get to the second level? I still don't see any stairs...

The system seemed to read my thoughts and spoke again.

"Please state your choice: attempt the next level or retire?"

Hmm. So all I had to do was speak aloud. I declared my choice immediately.

"I'll attempt the second level."

"Choice confirmed. You will now be transported to level two."

Like usual, the white glow surrounded my body. The teleportation spell activated and before I knew it, I was dropped in a different location.

"What is this place?" I asked the air.

This level was made of nondescript tile that stretched two hundred meters in every direction—the total opposite of level one's endless nature. I was astounded.

This dungeon really is different from the others. It's hardly a tower at all. Each floor is like a completely different location.

I didn't have the luxury to stand there and mull things over, though.

"What's the next quest? I don't see monsters anywhere," I said. The system responded to my voice once again.

"The second-level quest is the Reflect Knight. Defeat the target," it said. The explanation was short and sweet. Compared to level one's quest, it sounded easy, but maybe that belied how powerful this enemy would be.

Across from me, a white glow resembling the teleportation spell lit the space, then formed a knight clad in silver armor. The fine details were different, but its armor, stance, and general presence resembled the Nameless Knight.

"Is that the Reflect Knight?" I used Appraisal on it. My eyes widened at the text on the display. "Are you kidding...?"

REFLECT KNIGHT

LEVEL: 6,604

A knight created with stats copied from the adventurer Amane Rin. Failed to copy primary skill.

REFLECT SWORD

A sword created with the abilities copied from Sword of the Nameless Knight.

RECOMMENDED EQUIP LEVEL: 6,000

ATTACK +6,000

When an enemy (human or monster) is of a higher level than the wielder, all parameters except HP and MP increase by 56% each.

"It copied my stats *and* Nameless's too?! Oh, yeah, the system input my status into the tower!" It said as much when I maxed out the tenth dungeon for my Dungeon Traveler title. "I didn't expect it to be used *this* way though."

I drew Nameless and faced off against the Reflect Knight.

"Now, how are you going to atta—"

I didn't get to finish. The Reflect Knight shot forward, faster than I anticipated!

"Dammit!" I swore, evading the knight's sword by the thickness of a sheet of paper.

Yikes, did that ever make me reevaluate what I was up against. I grimaced as I wiped a bead of sweat from my forehead.

"So, you can move unpredictably... Well, you *do* have that sword."

The knight pointed the Reflect Sword at me—an identical copy of Nameless. When the system copied my stats, I was level 6,604. Thanks to level one of this tower, I'd grown to level 6,900. That meant the knight received the stat boost from his weapon, and I didn't.

"Well, gee, thanks. This isn't going to be easy..." I grumbled. Hunting stronger monsters was *my* specialty. That advantage belonged to my enemy now. "The Nameless Knight demonstrated monsters could benefit from the sword's effects, but I didn't expect to see it happen elsewhere."

Being on the other side of Nameless's effects made it feel all the more like a cheap weapon.

"The boost effects bring his stats close to level 10,000 or so, I think. That's about a 3,000-level difference. I'm at a major disadvantage."

As the truth of that sunk in, I dared to grin.

"That only makes this thing a worthy opponent. Thanks for giving me something meaty to chew on, Reflect Knight!"

And so our death match began.

The sound of our clashing swords—my Nameless versus his Reflect Sword—rang out across the floor. Thanks to his sword, Reflect Knight had the edge. Little by little, I was backed into a corner.

"He's strong...!" I grit out.

With the help of Superhuman Strength and Gale Wind, I dove into the fight with boosted power. Each skill raised my Attack and Speed by 60 percent to counter the Reflect Knight's 56 percent overall stat boost. I was at a disadvantage in my other stats, but it was what I could do to close the gap.

Then there was the other matter that Appraisal exposed. The Reflect Knight failed to copy my primary skill, but that meant it *didn't* fail to take the two skills I was using. My mind darted straight to the worst possible scenario.

If it decides to move faster, this'll get ugly real *fast!*

I was no stranger to stronger enemies like the Nameless Knight and orc general, but I always held the Speed advantage. That advantage was the key to victory each time. For some reason, the Reflect Knight wasn't utilizing it yet. I needed to stop it before it realized how important Speed could be!

"This'll be a mismatched combo, but something's got to change... Speed Sword!"

SPEED SWORD

A short sword made with a Blacksmith skill.

RECOMMENDED EQUIP LEVEL: 4,150

ATTACK +3,150

SPEED +1,600

I hefted the oversized Nameless in my right hand and the light Speed Sword in my left in an awkward dual-wielding style. Normally, I wouldn't attempt such a feat, but 'normal' did not apply to this situation.

Weapons and skills had two types of effects: active and passive. Passive effects worked in the background, while active effects only worked under specific circumstances. If I equipped Speed Sword, I gained an active effect of +3,150 Attack. But the effect only worked if I attacked with Speed Sword. It didn't add Attack to other types of movement, like kicks or attacks with Nameless. On the other hand, the +1,600 Speed boost was passive and activated as soon as I equipped it.

Speed Sword had a shorter reach than Nameless, but I ignored that. It wasn't like I expected to land any attacks with it. The purpose of equipping it was to improve the difference in Speed between me and the Reflect Knight, nothing more.

The Reflect Knight still surpassed most of my stats, but as long as I evaded, I had a chance. The passive Speed boost enabled me to stay on the defensive while I searched for an opening. The problem was *how* to counterattack.

The Reflect Knight didn't just have his Attack and Speed boosted, his Defense was as well. Half-hearted attacks wouldn't leave a scratch on him. There had to be something—just one thing—that I had over the Reflect Knight.

Realization sparked in the back of my mind. I did have one more asset.

"That's it!" I said. The next time I parried a strike, I put my plan into action.

"Taste *this*!!!"

I stashed Nameless into Item Box, swapped it for an Exploding Stone, and set it off. Monsters hated the white smoke; thanks to that, the Reflect Knight whirled away in disgust.

The Reflect Knight didn't have my items—which made them my ultimate trump card. It was a dirty trick, but it wasn't like I cared whether I won this fight fairly.

Hidden in the smoke, I whispered, "Evasion."

> **EVASION LV 4**
> Uses MP to erases the user's presence from the perception of nearby humans and monsters.

The success rate of Evasion on beast-type monsters was low due to their keen sense of smell, so I hadn't used this skill many times. But this enemy was no beast, so it might be the one move to help me the most.

When the smoke cleared, the Reflect Knight glanced around, having lost sight of me. Evasion worked—time to strike back.

I sprinted to the Reflect Knight's opposite side. Hidden with Evasion, it was best to run at max speed and put some distance between us. In a few seconds, I reached the end of the floor. I successfully put over one hundred meters between us, but that only lasted momentarily.

Huh...

A sense of foreboding sank over me, shapeless and chilling. It almost felt like making contact with someone else's mana, but no one else was there. That meant *he* did something—a very specific something.

He used Enemy Detection.

Out of my plethora of skills, that was the only one that spread mana into the surroundings. He was using it to search the floor for me. My speculation was confirmed when the Reflect Knight abruptly turned in my direction.

"Found me already, huh?" I said.

He ran for me at a high speed. I raised Nameless and Speed Sword. Evasion hadn't even held for ten seconds. The Reflect Knight howled wordlessly.

"Nice try!" I retorted.

He must've used Superhuman Strength and Gale Wind at the same time to power the swing of his sword because again, I dodged by a hair's breadth. When an opening appeared—

"Got a present for you," I said, and activated another Exploding Stone. The smoke enveloped us both, obscuring our vision.

"Evasion."

I erased myself and circled around the floor without stopping. The Reflect Knight used Enemy Detection a second too slow and chased after me. He roared in rage, like he didn't know where to place his fury.

Seeing him like that made me crack a smile. "*This* looks like it's working."

We repeated the same pattern a few times: me using Evasion and him using Enemy Detection to find me. I'd amassed a ton of Exploding Stones from my time in Kenzaki, so I wasn't afraid to burn through them. The hour-long fight turned into a game of cat and mouse, until a decisive moment finally arrived.

Out of the blue, the knight's movements slowed down. He stumbled in confusion, looking less like a dangerous enemy and more like a lost child.

"It finally worked!" I crowed, promptly dashing toward him. I pushed Speed Sword into my Item Box and swung forcefully with Nameless.

"Haaaaaaa!"

The knight attempted to counter, but without the speed he had before, I overwhelmed him and pressed him into a corner. With the force I put behind Nameless, his sword cracked and struck against his armor.

As for how it happened? It was all numbers. I ran out the clock until Superhuman Strength and Gale Wind drained his MP.

Of course, I was using those two skills too, but there were two reasons why his MP hit zero before mine. First, the Reflect Sword's ability to copy Nameless meant he received boosts to all parameters except HP and MP. Flip that around, and that meant he gained *no* additional HP or MP. Second, I'd invested the SP I gained from the tower's first level into Mana Boost, which kicked the skill level from LV 2 to LV 5. Ultimately, I had more MP to sacrifice.

The Reflect Knight borrowed my stats from *before* I started the Remote Magic Tower challenge: it didn't reflect the levels I earned while inside. Once I understood that, I knew draining his MP was the way to victory. Without access to Superhuman Strength and Gale Wind, the Reflect Knight was fallible. Hence, I wasted that time running around with Evasion. The wider the range of Enemy Detection, the more MP it drained. As I ran to the edges of the floor, he foolishly used Enemy Detection to find me over and over. Needless to say, that was an effective way to drain his MP to zero.

My plan worked. I wasn't going to let this hard-earned chance escape!

"Just give up!"

The knight reeled in surprise and attempted to block or strike back, anything to protect himself, but I'd already damaged his sword. *That* probably had something to do with the little skill level boost I sneaked in—raising Superhuman Strength from LV 6 to LV 7—while I used Evasion. It boosted my raw Attack stat too.

An enemy that couldn't use his weapon or his skills had no way to guard!

"Raaaaaaaah!"

This was my final stand. I attacked in quick succession, not allowing him a second to fight back. I shattered his sword further, broke through his armor, and targeted his joints. Inevitably, I struck a critical hit.

With his arm severed, the Reflect Knight dropped his weapon.

"This is the end!" I delivered the killing blow.

The knight groaned in pain as my sword struck, but he was soon silenced as I bisected his body. The two halves of the Reflect Knight split...and crumpled to the ground.

The system spoke immediately.

"Gained XP: Level increased by 26!"

"Level Two Quest: Reflect Knight is complete."

"Level-two takedown reward: Level increased by 100!"

Hearing the system announce my victory—and seeing the corpse of the defeated knight—I let loose a breath of relief.

"I actually managed to win," I marveled. I'd beaten level two.

> **LEVEL:** 6,900 → 7,026
> Total levels gained within the Remote Magic Tower: 422 (level two complete)

With level two behind me, I told the system to take me to level three, where a quest called Battle Trenches awaited me.

Unlike the first two levels, this level resembled a normal dungeon with its labyrinth-like structure. My directive was to find the right path and reach the goal. Simple stuff. The problem was the monsters that besieged me along the way.

> **SKELETON KNIGHT**
> **LEVEL:** 6,000
> An undead monster made entirely of bones. It does not flinch when it takes damage and engages its foes without reservations.

SKELETON MAGICIAN

LEVEL: 6,500

An undead monster made entirely of bones. It wields various types of magic.

I'd never seen one in the flesh (or lack thereof), but this dungeon was lousy with them. Skeleton magicians were the trickiest because even though level three was similar to a dungeon, the pathways were narrow. The lack of space turned every encounter into a life-and-death game of dungeon diving dodgeball. Worse, when one skeleton found me, they signaled the others and swarmed me with their allies. I honestly felt like I was about to die whenever they surrounded me from the front and rear.

But rest assured, I was fine amidst this danger! Because Dungeon Teleportation came to my rescue!

"Dungeon Teleportation!"

Once I learned the lay of the labyrinth, I used Enemy Detection to check whether skeletons skulked the surrounding tunnels, then followed up with Dungeon Teleportation to avoid the fight altogether. Only there was one problem: the labyrinth spanned much farther than what I was used to. No matter how many times I used Enemy Detection to test the boundaries, I couldn't find the goal anywhere.

"Though, I think I have an idea..." I said to myself.

I used Enemy Detection again and found a high number of monsters waiting in one particular direction, as if they were stationed to protect something. That suggested the goal waited just past them.

"I don't know if Dungeon Teleportation will skip me past *all* of them, but I have to try."

Armed and ready, I trekked in their direction with Evasion active. Some monster encounters were inevitable, but I killed them swiftly and slipped by before they could call for their allies. Eventually, I reached the place I'd searched for.

"Found it!" I declared with satisfaction.

This labyrinth was a complicated one, but the path through ultimately amounted to a single pathway of several hundred meters. Beyond that waited a sparkling room—the goal. Before the quest began, the system sent me a mental image of what the goal looked like, so I doubted this was a trick of some sort. Regardless, it was well guarded, and only a small army of skeletons crowded the pathway.

"There isn't much space between here and the goal...but I figured it wouldn't be that easy."

They were clustered in creaking groups of ten or more each, and if I didn't push past them, I wouldn't reach the goal.

Behind me, hundreds of monster footsteps rumbled.

"Shoot, is that sound what I think it is?!"

Wasn't I still using Evasion? Something or someone must've tipped them off to my location.

They're about to pin me down. I have to move, now!

I bolted. I would break through before the reinforcements could reach me!

With Evasion on my side, I rapidly cut through the skeletons. They startled and looked around, but I left their defensive line in a trail of confusion behind me. Once tipped off to my presence, the next line of skeletons swung wildly, as if searching for me. I needed to take them down before they wised up and launched magic.

By the time I thought of that, I'd only defeated half of them, so it wasn't long before my fears came true.

About thirty meters ahead, a skeleton magician launched a massive, pathway-consuming fireball at me. I groaned in frustration. But instead of stopping, I whispered, with impeccable timing:

"Dungeon Teleportation."

A few seconds later, I materialized on the other side of the fireball. "I'd call that plan a success!"

Honestly, I couldn't believe teleporting to the opposite side of a magic attack worked as a dodge method; my skill was much faster than it used to be! With that edge on my enemies, I plunged forward.

"Level Three Quest: Enemy Trenches is complete."

"Level-three takedown reward: Level increased by 150!"

Whew! I safely conquered level three.

I continued on to level four, where a quest called "The Jewel of the Death Beasts" awaited me. That quest was so difficult, it *had* to be designed to kill me.

LEVEL: 7,026 → 7,191
Total levels gained within the Remote Magic Tower: 587 (level
 three complete)

◆ ⌃ ◆

Stepping into level four made me shake my head in disbelief at the sight before me.

"What is this place?" I said in awe.

A one-meter-tall pedestal with four round cavities was positioned in front of me. The cavities suggested something belonged inside them. But it wasn't the pedestal that surprised me. Past it waited an unreal sight that resembled a video game far more than anything in real life—a tunnel about fifty meters wide and three hundred meters deep with *hundreds* of magic attacks flying back and forth.

I couldn't see clearly from so far away, but it looked like the magic stopped at the end of the path. Until that point, the tunnel was alive with a flurry of fire, spears of ice, lightning strikes, and fierce cutting winds. Each spell had enough power to completely tear apart a person's body.

"This is bizarre by itself, but what about those things...?" I muttered as I glanced around. Four giant doors, two on each side, framed the pedestal. Mana of oppressive density overflowed from inside the four doors. The aura was so powerful, it was easily three times stronger than any enemy I'd faced.

"Clearly, the difficulty here is completely different from level three...! What's this level playing at?"

The system heard my doubts and spoke.

"Level Four Quest: The Jewel of the Death Beasts. Breach the magic barrier and reach the designated location."

"Each door on level four contains a monstrous beast: The Death

Beast of Fire, the Death Beast of Ice, the Death Beast of Lightning, and the Death Beast of Wind, respectively. Each beast guards a jewel. Steal the jewel and insert it into the corresponding hole in the pedestal. Doing so will stop the associated magic attacks."

"The Death Beasts are each level 50,000."

"This level grants special exception to those who wish to retire after the quest begins. However, should you choose to retire, you can never challenge the Remote Magic Tower again."

"Wait," I said. That was one shocking fact after another, but one stood out. "Did the system say *level 50,000*?!"

I received no answer from the pitiless system.

"Ugh. I need to calm down and analyze the information." I drew in a deep, steadying breath.

"Technically, the quest doesn't require me to *defeat* the Death Beasts. I just need to steal the jewels they protect...but to fight level 50,000 monsters? That's impossible."

Even Nameless's stat increases would barely cover a fifth of the difference. Not to mention, beast-type monsters would sniff me out if I used Evasion. I suspected my likely success rate was somewhere around zero.

"Wait—the system didn't say I *had* to steal the jewels either. The objective is to reach the end point. If I can endure the magic bombardment, I can make it through! If I could do something about the magic..."

I withdrew a small magic stone from my Item Box and threw it into the tunnel as a test. The barrage of spells swallowed it up and pulverized it into dust in less than a second.

"Nope, not happening!"

My magic resistance wasn't anything to boast about, so no way would I endure *that*. The Ring of Marou (True) helped somewhat, but the item wouldn't spare me from most of the damage. That left me with one option.

"This quest allows me to retire partway through, huh?" I considered.

Until now, I had to choose before the quest began. But if this option was on the table, that fact hung over my head like a threat: what if retiring from the challenge was created *for* this test? What if this was the system's way of telling me to throw my hands up and quit? That I had no choice?

If so, it wasn't wrong to send such a strong warning. This level presented me with monsters I couldn't protect myself from and powerful magic I couldn't survive without even saying 'good luck.' Maybe I should accept the system's warning and give up. But...

"I made a vow," I reminded myself.

I remembered my fight with the Nameless Knight. He was so much stronger than I was, but I didn't need to make the "right choice" to come out with my life intact. Call me a fool, but I swore then I'd decide my own terms and carve a path forward no matter what. Giving up wasn't in my vocabulary anymore!

"I'll do it," I declared. Even if the system prepared a whole dungeon just to kill me, my feet didn't know how to turn back. I didn't care if this was my greatest obstacle yet!

"You know what? I'll make it, *and* I'll complete this quest faster than anyone else in the world!"

About 250 seconds later, my victory came.

"Level Four Quest: The Jewel of the Death Beasts is complete."

"Level-four takedown reward: Level increased by 200!"

"I did it!" I whooped.

Leave it to Dungeon Teleportation to painlessly deliver me safe and sound to the other side of the tunnel of magic. I sensed that the system wasn't pleased with me, but that was probably my imagination. Yep, it was all in my head!

Thrilled as I was to complete the Level Four Quest, what the system said next amped me up further.

"The Jewel of the Death Beasts is complete. Now bestowing bonus reward."

"Hm? Bonus reward?"

A potion-type item materialized in front of me. *This* was the bonus reward? I used Appraisal to check the fine details.

COMPLETE RECOVERY POTION
Drinking this potion will fully restore HP and MP.
COOLDOWN TIME: 2 hours.

I couldn't believe my eyes.

"It fully restores HP *and* MP?!" I yelled. I couldn't help myself. Normal recovery potions restored set increments, such as one thousand points to HP and five hundred to MP. Extremely rare dungeon rewards offered potions that recovered HP in percentages, but even then, the most they'd restore was 50 percent. This one's effects neatly blew the others out of the water. No level requirement to use it either! High-level adventurers would pay millions of yen if I listed it for sale.

"Not that I plan to sell it! Potions are life for a solo player like me. I want to hang on to it."

At any rate, I was lucky to get a reward like this. I mean, I did a lot to unlock the Remote Magic Tower! I felt a little slighted at the lack of rewards thus far. Did it give me a bonus because I beat this particularly difficult quest?

I felt a little guilty for using Dungeon Teleportation to win so craftily, but on second thought... I didn't. Ha! I was really thrilled.

"I'll take a short break, then head up to level five!"

High on motivation from the unexpected reward, I proceeded to the next challenge.

Once I arrived, the system told me level five's quest was called The Wise Man's War. Based on the name, I figured the quest would test my Intelligence as opposed to the quests thus far, which tested my Strength. I thought the time had come for me to let my genius sing, so I was pumped. Unfortunately, what materialized in front of me was a giant monster.

It was simply an oversized gorilla, no matter how I looked at it. I used Appraisal and learned its name was Powerful Gorilla. So, yeah...literally just a really strong, huge gorilla.

It was also level 10,000—which made it stronger than anything I'd ever fought—but still. No magic, no armor, no weapons—just a gorilla. The system told me I'd get an additional reward for taking it down with my bare hands, so I gave it a shot. The Powerful Gorilla was muscular and nimble, which made it a tough opponent, but my punches landed faster and truer than this oversized beast could manage.

I had my skills to thank for my Speed advantage, because I dumped 3,500 SP into Gale Wind to boost it to LV 7. Furthermore, I used recovery potions after each chunk of damage. Just because I couldn't use a weapon didn't mean I couldn't use other items, so I grabbed from my stockpile.

At first, I thought this was a barbaric quest, but as we traded punches, I had the strangest sense that the gorilla and I were sharing the same world. As our muscles sang in harmony, the arduous path we'd walked to become capable of the force we put into the fight became crystal clear. The moment I recognized that, I felt connected to the Powerful Gorilla somehow.

I killed it in the end, but you know. There was something there! Really! The gorilla felt like it was a monster that this dungeon summoned to bestow knowledge upon me.

Oof. I think I got swept up in some phantom profoundness there. Full stop, time to move on.

"Gained XP: Level increased by 189!"

"Level Five Quest: The Wise Man's War is complete."

"Level-five takedown reward: Level increased by 250!"

"Bonus reward: Gained title, Wiser Wise Man."

Wow, so the bonus reward was a title! Wiser Wise Man, huh? My level-up speed could only increase from here.

AMANE RIN

LEVEL: 7,830   SP: 3,610

TITLES: Dungeon Traveler (10/10), Nameless Swordsman,
    Endbringer (ERROR), Wiser Wise Man

HP: 61,220/61,220   MP: 17,080/17,080

ATTACK: 14,930   DEFENSE: 12,480   SPEED: 15,790

INTELLIGENCE: 11,870 RESISTANCE: 11,910 LUCK: 11,320

SKILLS: Dungeon Teleportation LV 18, Enhanced Strength LV MAX,
    Herculean Strength LV MAX, Superhuman Strength LV 7,
    High-speed Movement LV MAX, Gale Wind LV 7,
    Purification Magic LV 1, Mana Boost LV 5, Mana Recovery LV 2,
    Enemy Detection LV 4, Evasion LV 4, Status Condition
    Resistance LV 4, Appraisal, Item Box LV 5, Conceal LV 1

WISER WISE MAN

A title granted to those who complete the quest Wise Man's War
    under particular conditions.
Grants 50% parameter increase to Attack, Defense, and Speed
    when no weapon is equipped.

Total levels gained within the Remote Magic Tower: 1,226 (level
    five complete)

TWO GIRLS IN SCHOOL UNIFORMS

MEANWHILE, *outside the Remote Magic Tower...*

Two girls in a certain classroom garnered attention from the rest of their classmates. One of them—Kurosaki Rei—sat in the row nearest to the window. Her beauty made many fall in love at first sight, but she carried an unapproachable and solitary air about her, as if she were a rare flower at the top of a mountain. No one dared speak to her, and she seemed to prefer it that way.

Except the second girl, who *did* dare. She shattered the silence around Rei without hesitation.

"Thanks for inviting me out last time, Rei-chan!" Yui bubbled.

Kasai Yui was cute enough to earn her fair share of crushes, but unlike Rei, she was open and kind to everyone. All of her classmates, regardless of gender, really liked her.

"...You're welcome," Rei replied.

In the past, the two girls had no reason to interact with each other. Something was different, and now, the curious ears of their classmates listened in to their conversation with keen interest.

The boys were especially curious, which was to be expected given the popular girls in question.

"Hey, Kasai-san and Kurosaki-san are talking!" a boy whispered.

"What do you think they're saying?" another asked.

"I'm dying to know...!"

Whether they noticed the boys watching or not, Yui and Rei talked as if they didn't.

"I keep thinking about how amazing you are, Rei-chan. I had no idea I was the only one of us that day without a unique skill. What does it take to be unique, anyway?"

Yui's shoulders slumped. Rei thought for a moment, then answered.

"No need to be upset. Rin said so before, remember? He said you have an abundance of talent as a healer. You don't need a unique skill for that."

"You mean it?! Huh. Rin-senpai had such nice things to say... tee hee. I'm kinda flattered."

"Grrr...!"

Rei tilted her head at Yui, then pinched her cheeks and stretched them.

"Whadd're you doin', Rei-hyan?" Yui asked. "Why my wheeeeeeks...?"

Rei released her without comment. It wasn't jealousy, that was for sure!

Suddenly, somewhere around them, someone said something about cute girls getting physical. Then a crash sounded, as if someone had fallen off their chair. Rei pretended she imagined the fuss.

Meanwhile, Yui reminisced like nothing had happened. "Thinking back, my senior guildmate said I'm a talented healer too. Maybe I should believe her."

"Senior guildmate?"

"Yeah! We're only two years apart but she's so strong, cool, and kind that you wouldn't believe it! She's gorgeous too!"

"It sounds like things are proceeding well with your guild. That's great."

"He he he, thanks, Rei-chan! With your party disbanded, are you going to keep soloing? What do you think about joining a new guild or party?"

"...I've considered it. Going solo is challenging. The fact that Rin can do it is rather unusual."

"Well, Rin-senpai is in a league of his own!" Yui declared.

"That's definitely true."

The girls continued their gossip about Rin and began to giggle. Yui then sat up abruptly, as if a thought had donked her on the head.

"Hey, Rei-chan! If you're debating where to plant your roots, I have a suggestion..."

Yui's eyes sparkled as she explained her idea to Rei. Rei listened intently, leaning forward as her interest grew.

CHAPTER 4

THE KING OF LIGHTNING

I MOVED ON to the Level Six Quest: Ultra Evasion.

This one was perfect for me! I was trapped in a room that stretched fifty meters across. Magic attacks shot at me from every cardinal direction, and for three hours, I had to dodge every attack to complete the quest. Unlike level four, I didn't need fancy tasks to reach a certain point. All I had to do was dodge. With my Speed-focused build, as long as I got the timing right, I evaded just fine.

During the latter half of the quest, the magic attacks increased in number *and* speed. The window for escaping a direct hit shrunk dramatically. Twisting and leaping, I survived and thrived at the end of my stamina and reflexes until I somehow managed to run the clock out.

"Level Six Quest: Ultra Evasion is complete."

"Level-six takedown reward: Level increased by 300!"

"Those who complete Ultra Evasion receive a bonus reward."

"Oho! I get a bonus reward here too?" I said.

The level-six bonus reward was shaped like a piece of candy, small enough to grip with my fingers. I used Appraisal on it.

> **MAGIC REBOUND MEDICINE**
> Swallowing this medicine will reduce all magic-related damage by
> 99% for ten seconds.

"Another big-ticket item!" I remarked.

The ten-second time frame was a ding against it, but the defensive effect was so complete that it was better than a lot of other items. If I used this the right way, it could really save my butt. Too bad it only worked once.

"Okay, just gotta keep this ball rolling!"

After a nice long rest, I proceeded to the next level.

Level seven's quest tested stamina and patience—much like level one. I equipped Nameless and defeated a never-ending stream of monsters.

"Gained XP: Level increased by 1!"

"Gained XP: Level increased by 1!"

"Gained XP: Level increased by 1!"

Level one must have prepared me, because this time, I didn't struggle psychologically halfway through. I mowed down monsters without pause and passed the test with flying colors.

"Level-seven takedown reward: Level increased by 350!"

On level eight, a quest that challenged Intelligence again awaited me (if you could really count last time). I couldn't brute force the puzzle it wanted me to unravel, and solving it sucked up a lot of time. After a lot of head-scratching, I managed to complete the quest.

"Level-eight takedown reward: Level increased by 400!"

Level nine's quest was like level six, rigged with a barrage of magic attacks. Unlike level six, I was required to defeat several monsters over level 10,000. At least they weren't level 50,000!

Since equipping Nameless was back on the table, beating them should've been straightforward. Unfortunately, we were forced to fight in close quarters, so it proved the most difficult quest thus far. But what was I going to do, *lose*? Not a chance!

"Gained XP: Level increased by 73!"

"Gained XP: Level increased by 66!"

"Gained XP: Level increased by 58!"

That was the most experience I'd ever gained from fighting individual monsters. My level climbed higher and higher, faster than any of the speed leveling I'd done with Dungeon Teleportation, or any of the floors below me in the Remote Magic Tower. As the number increased, a surprise arrived.

"Level-nine takedown reward: Level increased by 450!"

"Bonus reward: Gained skill, Revitalize."

REVITALIZE LV 1

This skill activates automatically when HP is at 30% or lower. The more the user's HP lowers, the more parameters of Attack, Speed, and Intelligence increase.

A new skill. Nice! Receiving skills as rewards was rare, so I was grateful.

"Although, based on the description, I'd say it's better if I never use this skill," I said. Sitting at 30 percent HP was like playing with death. I hoped I'd never need it.

That little treat ended my time on level nine.

Only level ten remained.

I knew in my bones that a truly monstrous enemy—stronger than anything else I'd ever face—awaited me there. The time to meet it would come shortly. Carefully, I set about preparing.

> Total levels gained within the Remote Magic Tower: 3,376 (level nine complete)

With level nine and a good night's rest behind me, I tinkered with my SP before heading for level ten. I had 12,510 SP remaining. Which skill levels should I increase? I scanned the list until one caught my eye.

> **OBTAINED SKILLS**
> Dungeon Teleportation LV 18 → LV 19 (SP needed: 4,500)

"Dungeon Teleportation, huh?" I said.

Based on the previous SP requirements, LV 20 would probably

require 5,000 SP. Including the 4,500 I needed for LV 19, I'd spend 9,500 total.

I rocked left and right as I stared at the display. "Hrmmm. As much as I want it to reach LV 20, there's no guarantee it'll be useful in battle. I'd better save this milestone for after I leave the tower. Instead..."

I boosted Superhuman Strength to LV 9 and maxed out Gale Wind at LV 10. That left me with 3,010 SP, which I invested in Mana Boost, bumping it from LV 5 to LV 7.

There. Ready as I'd ever be.

"Onward to the final level. Better collect my wits."

The system acknowledged my declaration and activated the teleportation spell. When I opened my eyes, an infinite, dismal wasteland lay before me. Dark clouds hung low in the sky, full of menace. A dense charge of mana prickled across my skin. It felt like standing at the gates of hell.

A monstrous beast waited in the center.

It prowled the ground ferociously on four thick, sturdy legs. Its immense body was clad in black armor. It stood taller than the orc general and was several times longer, with muscles that bulged as if bound tightly by rope. The fangs and claws looked blade-sharp and durable as steel, and the size of that tail?

One hit from that thing would shatter the earth.

Its cunning yellow eyes flashed brightly and bored into me with visible malice.

Like no creature I'd ever heard, it roared, long and loud. Lightning fell from the sky with a crash as if answering the creature's call. I couldn't believe what I was seeing, but the system spoke in my head and confirmed the reality of it.

"Level Ten Quest: King of Lightning. Defeat this lightning beast to complete the quest."

The second I heard that, I used Appraisal on the monster.

KING OF LIGHTNING
LEVEL: 20,000

Simple, but *devastating* information.

"Ha! I see. No exits or side doors. The only way out is through," I said. "Fine then. I'll make it happen."

I drew Nameless and stared the intimidating lightning beast down.

"We've got this, Nameless. This is the last fight."

With everything on the line, my final battle within the Remote Magic Tower commenced.

AMANE RIN
LEVEL: 9,980
SP: 410
TITLES: Dungeon Traveler (10/10), Nameless Swordsman,
      Endbringer (ERROR), Wiser Wise Man
HP: 77,820/77,820   **MP:** 21,980/21,780
ATTACK: 18,859   **DEFENSE:** 15,800   **SPEED:** 19,800
INTELLIGENCE: 15,320 **RESISTANCE:** 15,410 **LUCK:** 14,620

SKILLS: Dungeon Teleportation LV 18, Enhanced Strength LV MAX, Herculean Strength LV MAX, Superhuman Strength LV 9, High-speed Movement LV MAX, Gale Wind LV MAX, Revitalize LV 1, Purification Magic LV 1, Mana Boost LV 7, Mana Recovery LV 2, Enemy Detection LV 4, Evasion LV 4, Status Condition Resistance LV 4, Appraisal, Item Box LV 5, Conceal LV 1

SWORD OF THE NAMELESS KNIGHT
A sword used by the Nameless Knight.
RECOMMENDED EQUIP LEVEL: 8,500
ATTACK +8,500
When an enemy (human or monster) is of a higher level than the wielder, all parameters except HP and MP increase by 80% each.

The lightning beast was more massive than any monster I'd ever encountered. Due to its size, it would be difficult to aim for any vital organs around its head and body, at least right away. First, I'd make use of my speed to stay clear of its four long legs, tangle its limbs, and watch its stance crumble.

Well...that was the plan, but it fell apart almost immediately. Instead, it snarled and lunged for me faster than that hulking body should allow.

"Dammit!" I cursed.

Nameless's passive effects were in play, and Gale Wind was at full force, but my speed didn't guarantee victory. The lightning beast reared up on its hind legs. I barely dodged the blow that followed. I put distance between us and recovered my stance, but the beast growled and stalked toward me, undeterred.

"A follow-up attack?!" I cried, bewildered. The way this beast maneuvered its body defied the laws of physics. It landed smoothly and lunged in a whirl of claws and teeth, as if it understood the concept of multihit combos. I had to dance around, constantly on defense.

In the middle of evading, I saw a way to turn the tables.

"Now!" I shouted.

The window of opportunity was small, but I didn't let it go. I slipped past its outstretched claws and ducked under its forelegs, where I swung Nameless upward.

What happened next struck *me* with disbelief, rather than the beast. As my aggressive strike collided with the lightning beast's stomach, a noticeable *tink* sound crackled above the noise of battle.

"How—"

I panicked.

I knew the lightning beast's hide would be tough. A level-20,000 monster wouldn't die in a single hit. But what was *that*? It sounded as if the blade had rebounded off an invisible barrier before it even reached the hide.

Invisible barrier?

The second those words entered my mind, I couldn't drop

them. I struck again, determined to use this chance, but the same thing happened.

Crack.

Wait. Was that sound—

The beast snapped at me, but I spun away with a grunt. In front of an enemy as strong as this one, I didn't have a spare second to think. The beast stomped furiously, trying to crush me. I dodged and backed out of range.

Wary of its unreasonably fast movements, I circled warily as I considered my next action. On the one hand, this monster was blocking all of my attacks to the point where even a direct hit didn't connect—but that wasn't necessarily how it would *always* be. When it blocked my second attack, I'd learned something. Upon a second look, my blade didn't rebound off the beast's body. It rebounded off something surrounding it. I didn't miss that cracking noise. Nothing else should've existed here but this beast, so what made the sound?

I had a theory.

An invisible shape around the lightning beast—it was cloaked in some sort of *defensive* barrier. The changing sound proved I was doing damage. The fact it cracked on the second hit meant the barrier wasn't impenetrable.

Ultimately, my theorizing didn't change what I needed to do.

I slipped past the swiping of the beast's front legs and slashed Nameless repeatedly. With my plan in place, I slammed my sword hard again and again. The lightning beast opened its mouth wide and roared at the sky, so loud it felt like it might shatter my eardrums. The roar itself was a hassle, but things were about to get serious. Answering the beast's call, a bolt of lightning fell from the sky—directly at me.

I sensed the mana and leapt out of the way in the nick of time. Lightning struck and scorched the ground where I'd been standing. The reverberations shook through me.

"No way..." I said breathlessly. I'd evaded the bolt of lightning by a fraction of a second. If that had struck me, I wouldn't have simply taken damage: it might've killed me in one shot. My body trembled from the thought.

"Too soon to be relieved!" I told myself.

The beast roared on and on. A litany of lightning attacks rained from above.

What could I do? I barely dodged the last attack, and my success came from pure instinct, not strategy. Sensing traces of mana before it struck wouldn't work every time.

Should I give up?

Of course not. This was no time for jokes! Back to being serious!

"If I can't always sense the traces of mana, I'll track the flow of mana more closely. Enemy Detection!"

I activated the skill, which allowed me to detect all mana within the designated range. Tracking it above my head cost a ton of MP, but I couldn't complain. It made the flow of mana clear and the lightning easier to evade. The problem was that I'd need to take this beast down before my MP ran out. Now was the critical time to find an edge.

"Here I go!"

As I evaded the lightning bolts, I beelined for the beast. As I closed in, it stopped roaring. Would the lightning harm it? No time to wonder. It snarled at me as I sped in with a yell, both of us brimming with speed and strength. It was stronger than I was, and it rivaled my speed. Nevertheless, the harsh battles I'd faced in the past taught me a lot about going toe to toe with a daunting foe.

I had a chance.

My first swing rebounded on the beast's defensive barrier, but the second made a noticeable cracking sound. The third one—*at long last*—shattered the barrier. I focused my subsequent attacks on that vulnerable spot. Quick with my sword, I slashed with abandon at the lightning beast's body.

Stronger. Faster. Stronger! Faster! I repeated the mantra as I swung my sword. At this rate, I would win!

The beast roared again, heedless of the fact I was cutting into its body. I kept Enemy Detective active to track the mana. With its help, I could dodge more lightning strikes easily, or so I thought.

Then the mana flow changed!

"What's going on?" I said with alarm. This strike wasn't manifesting like the others. Mana concentrated above the beast like a blazing sun, dozens of times stronger than the other lightning strikes. Did it intend to electrify itself to damage me?

"Argh!" No way I could block that. As frustrating as it was, I had to put some distance between us again. This way, the beast would likely cease the attack.

It didn't. Contrary to my every expectation, its raucous roar continued. Mana still gathered above its head. After building to a fever pitch, a hyper-powered lightning strike crashed down on the beast in a searing, bright bolt.

"That's a flashy way to kill itself," I muttered as I watched the cloud of dust billow around it. I couldn't help but scoff. I mean, it should've known the strike wouldn't hit me, right? Yet it didn't stop the attack.

At any rate, the blow it took was devastating. Even if it wasn't dead, it was on the verge of it.

The dust settled and revealed the fate of the lightning beast.

"...What?" The sight stunned me. "Hold up. What's this now...?"

I thought it would be scorched beyond recognition, but what stood there was something else entirely. Every wound I'd dealt to its body was healed, and if *that* was any indication, the defensive barrier was also fixed.

If that was the extent of the change, it would've been obnoxious but manageable. But unlike its previous form, lightning itself now cloaked the beast's body. The pressure and malevolence it emitted had increased several times over, like it could crush me without moving a muscle.

I used Appraisal without thinking. My instincts told me it must've gained attributes unlike anything I'd ever seen, and they were spot on.

LIGHTNING BEAST (FORM: KING OF LIGHTNING)
LEVEL: 25,000

I gasped. "Level *25,000*?!"

This was a death sentence.

It had taken everything I had to survive against a level 20,000 monster, but this? Another 5,000 levels on top of that knocked my survival rate below 1 percent.

Defeat.

Despair.

Death.

Negative words like those flooded my mind, but still—*still*, it was precisely because of that desperation that I grinned so defiantly.

"I get it," I said to the air.

The preceding quests, from level one through level nine, had tested my stamina, determination, and intelligence. I pushed them to the limit in order to succeed. Level ten was different. It was designed to be insurmountable, even if I gave the quest my all.

Did the system want me to die?

No, that couldn't have been it. The system only wanted one thing.

If I couldn't overcome this lightning beast even at my best, then it was clear what I had to do.

"I'll win anyway."

With unwavering willpower, I raised Nameless against it.

"Here we go, King of Lightning. I *will* surpass my own limits!"

◆ ⮝ ◆

I had no strategy for the battle that followed. The lightning beast overwhelmed me so thoroughly that even dodging was a struggle.

I clucked my tongue in frustration. All I could do before the might of this creature was run. Its speed surpassed mine, and each attack had the power to annihilate me. I evaded direct hits, but grazes alone stung with pain. Combined with the shocking sparks of lightning that cloaked its body, my HP fell by nearly one thousand points. At this rate, I'd be overrun. The beast moved so fluidly that I couldn't find openings to parry or strike back either.

Should I use Dungeon Teleportation to escape to the lower levels?

No, that wouldn't work. I needed 0.8 seconds at a minimum to activate it. In a fight this advanced, I couldn't buy that kind of time with a pile of gold. Evasion was all I had—but protecting myself wasn't enough.

"There!"

I saw the slightest opening during my next dodge and took advantage of it, one-handedly swinging Nameless to slice at the beast's right front leg.

"What?!"

To my literal shock, my sword betrayed me, rebounding with a sharp *thunk* off the defensive barrier and conducting a bolt right up into my body. It burned horribly, and for a split second, the world went white. At the same time, my HP dropped by three thousand points. The beast's attack didn't end just because I was in pain. Seeing my weakness, it gave chase and kicked with its powerful back legs.

I blocked in desperation, but the weight of the kick sent me flying and forced the air from my lungs. I rolled and rolled over the ground, bouncing and skidding until I lost momentum. My HP display showed 14,345/77,820 in the corner of my vision.

That attack wiped out over half of my HP.

Worse, my one ray of hope—the Ring of Marou (True)—cracked and broke, as if it couldn't endure such a powerful magic attack. I was *doomed*. One more hit like that and death would know me by name.

The lightning beast ran at me as if it meant to make the introductions right away.

"No...!" I choked out.

I dragged my battered, bloodied body off the ground and attempted to retreat, but then I realized something. At that speed and with my body aching, I probably couldn't dodge.

Then what *could* I do? Just lay down and die?

Tch! Forget that!

"It can't end here!" I screamed.

I leapt aside with the last of my power, knowing it was probably futile. The beast stomped down with all four legs, delivering a shock wave that left a massive crater. Not four individual holes—an entire crater, as if a meteor had crashed into the battlefield.

Only then did it register that I was analyzing the destruction from a distance.

"What?"

I *had* dodged in time. I should've been pulverized beneath its paws. How did I escape...?

That's when I remembered the bonus skill I'd earned. "Revitalize kicked in!"

> **REVITALIZE LV 1**
> This skill activates automatically when HP is at 30% or lower. The more HP lowers, the more parameters of Attack, Speed, and Intelligence increase.

My HP was at 20 percent, which meant the skill had activated and granted me the speed I needed to escape. Based on feel, I guessed the boost amounted to 50 percent or so.

"And here I was trying so hard *not* to let this skill activate," I laughed. If nothing else, it saved my life.

The lightning beast quietly turned and analyzed me, as if it didn't expect me to evade that attack either. Meanwhile, I had to come up with a plan to spin the chessboard. Should I rely on Revitalize and attack with its effects in play? With my Speed *and* Attack stats boosted, I might compete with the beast.

"No, that's not true," I told myself.

I squinted at the enemy in front of me, thinking. Maybe that would work if I could defeat it in one hit, but the beast was cloaked in that annoying defensive barrier. I needed to land multiple hits before getting a real shot at the beast itself. Not to mention, it could use its lightning cloak to zap me back until my HP dropped to zero.

"Sucks to use it so soon, but I don't have a choice," I sighed, and withdrew the Complete Recovery Potion from Item Box.

I drank it in one decisive gulp, healing my wounds and fully restoring my HP and MP.

Back to the most pressing problem: thinking of an actual plan to beat this thing.

What can I do...?

The beast surpassed me in every way, and even if I attacked, that defensive barrier and lightning cloak would protect it. That giant, muscled body would pulverize me if I tried.

Predator and prey. That's what this dynamic felt like. No matter what kind of plan I dreamed up, none of them seemed feasible. Not a single weapon I owned could penetrate the beast's protections and wound the hide beneath without injuring me in the process.

"Except... for one."

A plan began to form in my mind. It was such an unbelievable plan, completely detached from reality, but it was a *plan*, nonetheless.

"Is it possible?" Logic pushed back at me, but instinct argued that this was the only viable option for survival.

The beast snarled and cut into my thinking time. It remained cautious, but it started to pace toward me. I could sense its intent—it wouldn't let me get away this time.

I made up my mind and lowered my stance. "I won't run away," I swore to myself. "I said I'd surpass my own limits!"

I plowed toward it. The beast roared and barreled at me.

The rest happened in a flash.

I raised Nameless to meet the beast's claws head on, and then—there! I used my momentum to slip under the claws instead of bringing Nameless down. Our paths collided.

Attack power wouldn't decide the outcome of this battle. Power *and* speed would. In this moment, the beast's speed was greater than mine. I wasn't simply swinging my sword hard— I was taking advantage of the *beast's* speed too! If I wasn't as strong or fast as the beast, I would use its own stats against it! This should break through its defenses in one strike!

"Take this!" I screamed.

I swung my blade with unprecedented force—

And sliced empty air.

"...Huh?"

I was sure I'd hit it. I must've. Confounded, I halted, unsure where the beast had vanished to.

"Above me?!" I shouted in horror as I realized. Just before my attack landed, it hit the brakes and propelled itself into a jump. The only reason it could manage that was because it had such unreal reflexes.

Now it was in the air, and the beast would use gravity to come down on those huge legs and crush *me*.

I held Nameless over my head as a shield, but defense was futile. It impacted me with the massive weight of it focused into its front right leg. I collapsed to the ground underneath its pressure. The force of it shattered the earth around me. As if I could possibly dodge that!

In the wake of the shock, I gasped. It pressed down harder, robbing me of air. My HP dropped by nearly half. Even if I tried to escape, in my breathless state, it would catch me.

The beast knew how royally screwed I was. That had to be why it didn't attack. Instead, it simply *watched*.

"Think I'm a goner, do you?" I spat with a sneer. Apologies to the beast, but I wouldn't let this battle end so cleanly.

It let out an animalistic howl at my disrespect, and lightning attacks once again rained down around us...yet I hardly took any damage. Why? Well, despite the tough situation, I had stopped for a small snack.

> **MAGIC REBOUND MEDICINE**
> Swallowing this medicine will reduce all magic-related damage by 99% for ten seconds.

I'd swallowed my Magic Rebound Medicine, the bonus reward from level six that nullified the majority of magic damage for ten seconds. In other words, ten seconds of free rein to slash the lightning beast at will. That it came out of our full-body clash unscathed was unexpected, but I wasn't hanging my hopes on that strike. When I jumped under its claws, I was tempting it to stomp me. That was part of the plan.

As for *why* I wanted to get stomped, it was simple: if the beast wanted to pin me down, it wouldn't move. It would hold me down with its foreleg and wait for the life to bleed out of me, as many seconds as it took.

That's what I was waiting for.

The beast let out a low growl as it watched me. It was probably wondering why I was taking my sweet time to die. Its expression shifted, as if it realized I was barely damaged.

With no time to waste, I swung Nameless at its other leg. It pushed down harder on my body in retaliation, but its action was too slow. The time I needed to activate my skill had passed.

Quietly but clearly, I said, "Dungeon Teleportation."

Dungeon Teleportation only worked when the destination was a dungeon I'd already visited. With it, I'd bypassed the Span and achieved outrageous leveling in a short time. It had other uses, like when I teleported into midair during my battle with the Nameless Knight and orc general. Those had their place, but *this* shiny new technique was different. It might be the simplest yet most effective use of all. I'd just never fought an enemy that put me in a position where I needed to imagine it.

Theoretically, my idea made sense—at least in the case of a monster so massive, it could swallow me whole.

I spoke to the beast one final time, from *inside* it, where not a single ray of light reached...for now.

"The inside of your body is *technically* inside the dungeon, you know."

I swung hard and cut the beast open from the inside. Its vulnerable guts vibrated as it howled in pain. As I'd hoped, the defensive barrier did nothing to protect its internal organs.

Man, the struggle I'd gone through made the effectiveness of this attack feel unreal, even if it was disgusting. This chance wouldn't come again, so I had to act decisively.

"Haaaaa!"

Several slashes later, I carved my way through the darkness of viscera, muscle, and skin. With one more slash of Nameless, I opened a gaping hole in the side of the beast's body. The cloudy sky above welcomed me back to the battlefield. The beast's defensive barrier was gone due to the massive damage I'd dealt to it.

To my surprise, lightning started crackling through its body.

"What in the world?!" I exclaimed.

It wanted to expel me from its body at any cost, and my Magic Rebound Medicine had worn off. I couldn't afford to take the hit, so I leapt into the air, still dripping the beast's blood. I gazed down at it below me while it looked back with bloodshot eyes. Furiously, it snarled.

"Nice try!"

It snapped at me like a rabid dog, but I swung to the side and used the momentum to chop into its neck. I finally had the upper hand. I ignored the beast's thrashing and focused myself down to a razor's edge.

Without the defensive barrier, my blade hewed smoothly into its hide. Fresh blood sprayed everywhere as it howled in pain. I pushed my blade fiercely into the beast's flesh.

We screamed in unison, a human and a beast on the brink of death, fighting with adrenaline and pure instinct. *This* could be the moment I surpassed my limits and not only won but *survived*. The beast's carcass would be my stepping stone to the next level!

The next thirty seconds stretched into an eternity. We struck each other, both damaging, until the gap between our movements widened. The gaping wound in the beast's abdomen and many cuts across its flank served to slow it down. On the other hand, my HP had fallen to the point where Revitalize kicked in again, increasing my speed.

The moment came—the precipice.

The beast abandoned its sense of preservation and launched itself at me in a tornado of teeth and claws. Nowhere to go except up! I launched myself into the air with a kick. The beast's last-ditch attack crashed into the place where I was seconds before. I gripped Nameless with both hands and cleaved it into the beast's head!

"This is it!!!" I shouted, putting my heart and soul into drawing out something *more* from myself. Just another second, another centimeter, another breath.

The blade sunk deeper and deeper, until the King of Lightning's ferocious growl quieted into a pitiful rumble—then silence.

Slowly, the beast's body slumped.

Gravity took over, and I fell to the ground. I rose abruptly on shaky legs, stepping into stance with Nameless raised and ready to strike again.

It wasn't necessary.

The system spoke in my head, signaling the quest was over.

"Gained XP: Level increased by 1,232!"

"Level Ten Quest: The King of Lightning is complete."

"Level-ten takedown reward: Level increased by 500!"

"All-quest takedown reward: Level increased by 1,500!"

For the first time since our fight ended, it registered that I'd *really* defeated the lightning beast.

"...It's over."

Wait—I didn't just defeat the beast. I beat the whole extra dungeon.

I conquered the Remote Magic Tower!

AMANE RIN

LEVEL: 13,212   SP: 32,710

TITLES: Dungeon Traveler (10/10), Nameless Swordsman, Endbringer (ERROR), Wiser Wise Man

HP: 35,850/104,020   MP: 15,080/28,100

ATTACK: 24,720   DEFENSE: 20,840   SPEED: 25,820

INTELLIGENCE: 20,520   RESISTANCE: 20,600   LUCK: 19,620

SKILLS: Dungeon Teleportation LV 18, Enhanced Strength LV MAX, Herculean Strength LV MAX, Superhuman Strength LV 9, High-speed Movement LV MAX, Gale Wind LV MAX, Revitalize LV 1, Purification Magic LV 1, Mana Boost LV 7, Mana Recovery LV 2, Enemy Detection LV 4, Evasion LV 4, Status Condition Resistance LV 4, Appraisal, Item Box LV 5, Conceal LV 1

SWORD OF THE NAMELESS KNIGHT

A sword used by the Nameless Knight.

RECOMMENDED EQUIP LEVEL: 10,000 (MAX)

ATTACK +100%

When an enemy (human or monster) is of a higher level than the wielder, all parameters except HP and MP increase by 100% each.

Total levels gained within the Remote Magic Tower: 6,608 (Final result)

CHAPTER 5

BLOODLUST EATER

WITH THE LIGHTNING BEAST'S massive body still sprawled at my feet, I opened my stats display and found that I'd broken level 10,000.

"Can't believe I reached this milestone..." I said, amazed. "I'm a long way away from becoming top-ranked, though."

Time felt like the main obstacle, which was natural. With the way the system worked, the ones who had the most time on their side became the strongest. However, little by little, I was catching up.

"Hey, shouldn't I receive some level-up rewards for defeating the whole tower? If not, this will feel super underwhelming."

As if hearing my griping, the system rang out.

"Conquest of extra dungeon: Remote Magic Tower has been confirmed."

"Now dispensing three conquest rewards."

"First conquest reward: the 'Battle Barrier' skill."

"Battle Barrier skill?" I repeated.

Huh. My first reward was a new skill, then. I opened my stats display and checked Battle Barrier's effects.

> **BATTLE BARRIER LV 1**
> By draining MP, this skill creates a mana barrier around the target. (Note: The strength and duration of the effect changes according to skill level.)
> **COOLDOWN TIME:** 60 seconds.

"Is this like the barrier the lightning beast used?" I pondered. If it was, this skill was an excellent one, and it matched my fighting style too.

Lots of protective skills that boosted Defense and Resistance parameters existed, but they only decreased damage. They didn't prevent pain or stop enemy attacks from staggering an adventurer's fighting stance and creating vulnerabilities. Battle Barrier could solve both problems for me.

"Based on what I saw from the lightning beast, the Battle Barrier totally blocks damage until the barrier breaks. That means it would be safe for me play around more with high-risk, high-reward gambits! This expands my battle options a ton!"

I punched the air enthusiastically.

Oops. Couldn't get lost in my excitement just yet. "I'm supposed to receive three rewards, aren't I? The other two ought to be on par with this one."

I waited with excitement while the system spoke again.

"The second reward shall be determined based on analysis of the

conqueror's stats and the methods used to defeat the Remote Magic Tower."

"*Conqueror analysis complete.*"

"*Authorized classification: Bloodlust Eater. Odds of acquiring this classification are 0.1%.*"

"*Now manifesting qualifying item.*"

"Uh, 'Bloodlust Eater'...?" I echoed.

The unsettling term had to take a backseat while glowing white mana gathered in front of me. A few seconds later, the vague shape of an item appeared within the light.

"...Is this the second reward?" I tried to activate Appraisal immediately—but an unusual phenomenon beat me to the punch. An ear-grating *bzzzt* sounded.

"Wh-what the heck?!"

I covered my ears, but it didn't help because the system spoke directly to my mind. What was happening here?

"*Error detected.*"

"*The conqueror has not met all conditions to receive the third reward.*"

"*The third reward cannot be granted.*"

"What?!" I screamed in frustration. I worked *so hard* to defeat the Remote Magic Tower, and the system was telling me I couldn't receive every reward?

"Hey, System! What's this about?" I yelled. "Are you mad I bent the rules midway through? I'm sorry, okay? Can't I have my third reward since I apologized? Hello?!"

My voice echoed into silence. Just when I was about to give up, the system continued as if offering an olive branch.

"A consolation prize will be granted instead."

"The consolation prize will be information about the dungeon."

"Conqueror will receive information deemed most valuable to them based on analysis of their data."

"What *kind* of information about the dungeon?" I asked.

No way the system would respond to me directly, but this *was* an unexpected turn of events. A modest hope welled in my chest. I knew certain dungeon secrets that no one else knew—the existence of the Dungeon Traveler title, the purpose of the Remote Magic Tower—but there was an overwhelming amount of unknown information about dungeons in general. What dungeons were, why people were given levels and skills, the mechanisms behind their appearance twenty years ago...so many questions remained up in the air. I might get a peek beyond the tip of the iceberg.

"Conqueror analysis complete."

"Consolation prize will be awarded."

Before I could even hold my breath in anticipation, a rectangular hologram materialized in front of me. Curiously, it looked like I'd get the information via an image.

"Okay, what've you got for me?" I asked, expectant. A picture formed inside the rectangle, but the sight it revealed was the last thing I predicted. My eyes widened and I blurted, *"What?!"*

A few hours earlier.

"Why isn't he back?!" Hana shouted at the empty living room.

It was several days since Rin left, and he still hadn't contacted her, which thoroughly soured her morning. Her cheeks puffed into a pout. She couldn't help herself. After all, it was the day she had dungeon practice.

"I know he said he might not make it, but I never thought he *really* wouldn't. He hasn't even called! Jeez, he left me in a pickle." It was already time to go. "I'll send him a text for now, but once he gets home, I'm gonna go *off* on him, for real."

Hana grabbed her things in a hurry and left for Sumifuku Dungeon, where the group was scheduled to meet.

Once at Sumifuku, Hana noticed a much smaller group had gathered than the last time. Those who'd failed to obtain stats had been plucked out of the class like dandelions. Most of those who made it had brought escorts. The rest of the people at the dungeon were normal adventurers going about their everyday dives. The dungeon wasn't reserved for trainees like her.

Hana stood a short distance away, where she could see the new tower encroaching on the city skyline. It scraped past the clouds, so high the tip was hidden from view.

"That's gotta be a dungeon too," she mused. The tower had shot up out of nowhere just days ago within walking distance from Sumifuku. Experts suspected it wasn't a dungeon because they couldn't locate a Gate, but their research hadn't progressed far enough to say one way or another.

"I'd better worry about myself first. I need to put my best foot forward if I'm going to defeat a *real* monster today."

While Hana psyched herself up, a shadowy figure approached behind her.

"Good morning, Amane-san," the figure said. She turned.

"Oh! Umm..." She hesitated. She recognized him as the Dungeon Association staff member she'd met last time, but she had to search the corners of her memory for his name.

I remember!

"You're Yanagi-san, right? Nice to see you again," she greeted.

"Yeah. It's good to see you. Are you alone today?"

He probably wanted to know whether Rin was there. Hana smiled ruefully and nodded. "Yeah, I'm on my own. My brother's been away for a few days now, but he *did* teach me a lot before this, so I should be fine on my own!"

"I see... That's such a shame, isn't it?" Yanagi asked.

"Uh, yeah...?"

The conversation held a weird charge she couldn't quite explain, so she nodded again to confirm that yes, Rin wasn't there. During their exchange, the other Dungeon Association staff member—Katagiri—arrived to address the group. He and Yanagi were the only two staff members that she could see. With the number of participants so much smaller, they required less supervision, she supposed.

"We're about to begin the practice session, everyone," Katagiri said. "Unlike last time, the monsters on the deeper levels are stronger, but you have no need to worry. We'll be with you, so just relax and do your best."

He ushered trainee after trainee into the Gate, like ants scurrying into a hole. Hana hustled over so she wouldn't fall behind.

"It really is a shame…" said Yanagi behind her. But he said it so softly that the words never reached her ears.

Hana estimated it was about thirty minutes since they'd entered Sumifuku. The group had descended to level three. A host of monsters lurked in the shadows. Unlike the wimpy lesser slimes on level one, these monsters would have some fight in them. As she thought that, a monster formed from bones shuffled before Hana and the group.

Katagiri spoke. "This monster is a skeleton, as you can see. Anyone with stats can defeat one. For this training exercise, everyone must defeat a skeleton without assistance!"

Escorts were forbidden from helping? Not that the rule affected her. She was alone.

"Okay." She hoisted her borrowed sword. "I've got this!"

Though it was the same sword, it felt lighter than last time. Today, she could swing it easily. Her stats had affected her already.

She considered if she should use magic. She didn't possess any magic-type skills, but with Stock, she *could* borrow one. That said, she decided to take Rin's advice and hide her skill.

One by one, Hana and the others took turns defeating skeletons under the watchful eyes of Katagiri and Yanagi. Like Katagiri said, the skeleton was weak and easy to defeat for Hana despite her lack of battle experience. Katagiri watched her kill the skeleton, then nodded with satisfaction.

"Well done, everyone," he said. "You won't have any issues facing a battle with monsters for the time being. Next, we're going to teach you more details about the adventurer lifestyle as we move—"

The girl beside Hana gave a high-pitched, tremulous scream that echoed through the dungeon. She pointed in the opposite direction as her whole body shook. Hana turned to where she was pointing, and her eyes widened with horror. Three frightful, imposing shapes were before them.

"What are those?" she asked carefully.

A first glance, they appeared to be trees, but as she looked closer, their forms were human-like as well. They must be monsters. With predatory intent, they marched toward the group. She didn't need a wealth of dungeon diving experience to know these monsters were different from the lesser slimes and skeletons—they were *powerful.*

"Treants?! Why would level 5,000 monsters be in a dungeon like this one?!" Katagiri hollered from the opposite side of the treants. The treants had the trainees cornered, and all at once, everyone registered how hair-raisingly dangerous this unusual situation had become.

One of the treants moved with frightening speed and swiped at Hana and her group. The trainees froze, too shocked and confused to run.

"Watch out!" Yanagi shouted.

He sprang between Hana's group and the treant, blocking the attack with his dagger. He narrowly saved their lives.

Katagiri's voice then boomed across the space. "Fire Spear!"

A massive spear formed from fire shot out of his hands and struck the treants with a burst of incandescent heat. Somehow, the treants remained standing.

"Impossible!" he exclaimed. "They're weak to fire! How is it barely burned?!"

The direct hit only left a few scorch marks on the treants. Hana picked up on the panic in his words.

"What's happening?" she asked.

"Even the Association people can't beat these monsters!" another trainee said.

"That can't be true! What'll happen to us?!" someone else yelled.

Chaos, panic, fear—the emotions struck the group like a bus with the brake lines cut. For the first time in their lives, they stood on the brink of death, and they discovered that their bodies didn't *listen*.

Yanagi spoke above the crowd. "Katagiri-san! Get everyone above ground! I'll hold them off!"

"Out of the question! We should both stay and let the escorts take them up!"

"There could be other powerful monsters in here! Please, go with them! And—"

Yanagi vanished on the spot.

A second later, a dagger became visible as it slashed a treant at close range. The treant tried to swipe back, but Yanagi countered it nimbly.

"I'm a speed-focused adventurer!" he said. "I can take them on if I keep moving!"

"...Okay! It should take ten minutes to get above ground. If you can buy that time, come back to the surface!" he replied. "That's the plan, everyone! Follow me out! We'll do everything we can to protect you in this emergency!"

The trainees obeyed and chased after him.

I need to hurry! Hana thought.

She was unlucky enough to be on the opposite side of the room from Katagiri, so she trailed at the rear of the group. She ran as quickly as she could, but something snagged her ankle from behind and sent her tumbling to the ground.

"Wha—?!"

She looked down and found ivy curled around her ankle. It bound her, shackling her in place. With the vines wrapped so tightly, she couldn't even stand.

"Ivy?" she gasped. "Why would it grab me...?!" She frantically twisted around to see the departing group growing distant. "Get off of me, I need to follow them!"

As the ivy tightened its grip, the group kept moving without her. *I'll really be left behind,* she realized. "Hey, wait—"

The ivy slapped over her mouth, silencing her before she could call for help.

No! I can't stay here! The group will only get farther away! I have to untie this!

She desperately clawed at the ivy. In an instant, it went slack as if it lost all strength. As it fell away from her mouth, she coughed and gasped for air.

"Why did it fall—no, questions later. I need to get out of here!"

She had more misfortune in store. As soon as she stood to run, a wall shot up in front of her and blocked her way. No—it wasn't a wall.

It was a treant.

"Get back!" Yanagi ordered.

Hana reeled away. The treant struck hard at the ghost of her from a moment before. She panted with the effort of dodging. If she had moved a second later... Her body quaked thinking about it. Even with a deep breath, she couldn't ease the tremors.

Yanagi lashed out with his sword and knocked it to the ground, then approached her.

"Sorry," he said. "The treant changed direction, and I responded too late."

"...R-right," she said unsteadily.

"I know this is hard to hear, but the group is long gone. You'll have a hard time finding your way back alone."

"Oh, no...!"

Yanagi's shoulders raised slightly as his expression turned sympathetic. Hearing his words made Hana's heart race faster. If he was correct, she couldn't leave this location on her own. She'd have to risk her life to stay with Yanagi while he fought off the treants.

Terror threatened to drown her.

Something different, something like determination, lifted Yanagi's expression as he watched her. "Amane-san, I have a favor to ask you," he said slowly and deliberately.

"A favor...from me?"

She hardly believed what came out of his mouth next.

"Would you mind lending me your unique skill—Stock, that is—to help get us out of here?"

Honestly, she had no idea why he was asking. Stock could only copy another person's skill if it was LV 1. Worse, her stats would determine the power output, and she was low level. It would be difficult to make any use of the skill with limitations like that.

Wait.

How did he even know about Stock *anyway*? She'd hidden it.

Her hesitation must've shown in her body language because he became apologetic.

"I'm sorry. I used my Enhanced Intuition skill on the participants to ensure nothing went south during the first practice run. I overheard that you acquired a unique skill...and that you used Conceal to hide it. I knew you didn't do it to cause trouble, and it was my bad for eavesdropping, so I just kept an eye on you."

Hana didn't like knowing he'd eavesdropped on her. Still, he'd taken her safety into account and protected her. She couldn't blame him too much, since she was the one who wasn't forthright about her stats in the first place. Either way, they could hash that out later. She needed to clear up something.

"You're right about what it does, but Stock *doesn't* borrow the power behind the skill it copies. I don't think I can help you."

"Yeah, I suspected, but you don't need to worry about that."

"Why not?"

"We can get into it when we're not in danger. For now, will you copy my Bullet skill?"

"O-okay!"

If Yanagi had a plan to get around her limitations, she'd cooperate. Worry still clouded her face, but she placed a hand on him.

"Stock!" she commanded, and his skill information popped into her head.

BULLET LV 1

A skill that releases a ball of mana that contains decimating power. Power output is determined by percentage of MP spent.

"The 'Percentage of MP spent?'" she read, cocking her head at the unfamiliar description.

Yanagi nodded. "This skill powers itself regardless of the user's stats. You can determine how much punch in your output based on the *percentage* of MP you pay."

Hana remembered something Rin had told her: some skills didn't depend on stats to deal damage. Bullet must've been one of them.

"I'll create an opening, so you use all your MP to activate Bullet. The treants are around level 8,000. If you use Bullet at 100 percent power, I think you can take out these monsters."

"Why not activate Bullet yourself?" she countered.

"I've used 20 percent of my MP to fend them off. You can make it more powerful than I can right now."

Hana had only used a sword that day, so he was right; her MP was full. Maybe it was better if she went on offense. Regardless of what he said, was she truly prepared to take on such a major role? The pressure of the situation weighed on her. If she didn't fight, they could both die. She had to try!

"Okay," she agreed. "I'll do it."

"Thank you. The treants are regrouping, so wait for my signal!"

The treants launched at them just as they finished talking, as if they'd waited for the conversation to end. Their thrashing branches and curling vines hurtled toward the two of them.

"Haaa!" yelled Yanagi as he swung his short sword. He deflected a branch at amazing speed and followed it with an elaborate dodge that seemed to strain him. He must be struggling to make sure the attacks didn't reach her.

I can do this.

With the skill copied, the knowledge of how to use it bubbled up inside her. She held out her hands in front of herself and collected her focus. One moment, then another—until the timing was right. Over a dozen branches and vines flew at Yanagi, but he narrowly sidestepped them. The attacks struck the ground. The treants stopped briefly to recover.

"Bullet!"

An ominous shot of black mana fired from her hands and struck the treants. They couldn't evade, and when the mana impacted, it utterly obliterated them. The sound of crumbling bark raining on the ground filled the room.

The system spoke inside Hana's head.

"Gained XP: Level increased by 452!"

"...I beat them?" she asked.

If she gained levels, she must've. But she'd borrowed the power to kill them. Even though the treants were dead, it didn't feel like *her* victory.

Oh, right. Where's Yanagi-san?

She searched around for him. If he was happy with her performance, she'd feel better about winning. It wasn't hard to find him. He was smiling down at the treants' corpses, or what remained of them. She placed a hand on her chest and breathed a sigh of relief.

"We did it, Yanagi-san!"

"Sure did." His smile turned more sinister. "It was worth all this planning."

Tentatively, she repeated his name. "...Yanagi-san?"

He sucked in a breath, as if returning to himself. His smile softened just as quickly as it had prickled.

"Yes, Amane-san? Did you say my name?"

"N-no. Um, I'm glad we defeated them."

"So am I. Everything went well, thanks to you."

He didn't elaborate.

Did I imagine that? Hana wondered.

They walked together after that. Yanagi smiled the whole time, but something was off about him. She clenched her hands by her sides.

Without warning, Yanagi spun toward her.

"...Are you two okay?!" echoed a voice in the distance. He was still a ways away, but Hana recognized it as Katagiri. Yanagi looked away from Hana and spotted him. She watched his profile, and saw that for a split second, his smile fell.

That unsettled feeling buzzed inside her again.

"You're back, Katagiri-san," Yanagi said. "How's everyone else?"

"They're on standby above ground, but I did a head count and realized I was one short. You managed to protect her. Thank goodness for that." He saw the destruction behind them. "I imagine you defeated them, given the treant corpses? I'm surprised. My magic hardly did any damage!"

"Amane-san's power managed to save the day."

"What? She's a newbie who doesn't have her qualifications, but she helped in battle? I have a hard time believing that."

"She did. She possesses a promising unique skill."

...What?

Yanagi spilled her secret like it was the most natural thing in the world! While she panicked internally, they continued their conversation.

"A unique skill?!" Katagiri exclaimed. "I didn't notice that when I checked her stats. I confirmed them myself!"

"She seems to have hidden it on purpose."

"What?" he replied with shock. Hana was yelling the same thing in her own mind. She never expected Yanagi to expose her secret so casually.

"Y-Yanagi-san! You just..." she trailed off.

"Oh, I'm sorry," he replied. "I should've asked your permission before I told Katagiri-san. I figured it would be fine."

"You 'figured', huh?!" she asked incredulously.

Yanagi scratched the back of his head as if he was embarrassed. "Yes, I did. I mean, come on." He smiled innocently, as if he was the kind of person who wouldn't hurt a fly and spoke casually, like they were discussing the weather. "It's not like Katagiri-san will leave here alive anyway."

He flipped his dagger and drove it directly into Katagiri's chest.

"...Huh?" Katagiri said.

"...What?" Hana gasped. What was she seeing?

Katagiri gaped down at the sword plunged into his chest. "Y-Yanagi, what are you—"

"Oops, I almost forgot! You possess the strongest magic skill there is, don't you, Katagiri-san? As distasteful as stealing is, I'll be taking it."

"You...what...?" he choked out. "What are you...thinking? Picking me...to plunder from..."

Katagiri never finished his sentence. The light left his eyes, and he slumped to the ground. A human being had died—right in front of her.

No way, no way, no way... This can't be real!

Her mind scrambled as she tried to process the sight. It had to be a trick. Meanwhile, the man responsible for everything sighed as if he was bored.

"He should've stayed above ground," Yanagi said. "*Idiot.* He could have lived. Oh, well. I'll say a monster killed him and leave him for them to eat—Oops! Almost forgot my primary objective."

Yanagi turned his icy gaze to Hana. She froze as if the temperature had dropped far below zero.

"On that note," he said, "I need you to die too, Amane Hana."

As Yanagi declared his intention to kill her, Hana's thoughts screeched to a stop as if they'd driven into a brick wall—then flailed as they tried to claw out of the wreckage. She fumbled to speak.

"Y-you're going to murder me...that's really what you're saying?" she asked.

"Yes, I am. Sorry, but the matter *is* settled. There's no point to resisting"

He stepped closer. Hana could barely budge.

"Why are you doing this?" she asked. "Do you hate me?"

Apparently unhurried, he stopped and considered her question. "Hate you? I could never. No, I'm quite grateful to you. Not many people would have a unique skill like Stock that's such a perfect fit for me."

"...Perfect *fit* for you?"

"Exactly. I'd feel bad if you died with unanswered questions, so allow me to explain," he said. "I have a unique skill myself. It's called Plunderer, and it allows me to steal one skill from anyone I kill. So, I'm going to kill you and steal Stock."

A unique skill. *Plunderer*—a skill of pure iniquity. The fact he wanted to use it on her made Hana shudder with fear.

That wasn't all—his earlier words rang out in her memory.

"Does that mean you *planned* this, even the monsters?" she asked.

"That's right. I used powerful monsters to isolate you, and now, I'll take this opportunity to kill you and blame it on the dungeon."

"But how?! You make it sound like you summoned the monsters—"

"Oh, I did! Heck, I can show you how."

"Huh?!"

Yanagi brightly waved his hand in the dungeon gloom. A monster—a treant—stepped out from a portal that manifested from nothing. It was just like one of the monsters they'd defeated. Hana, petrified, stayed silent. Yanagi nodded in satisfaction.

"Manipulating monsters requires a unique skill called Tamer. Truth be told, it wasn't mine originally. I killed the person who had it first!"

"Tamer?! You didn't!" The skill name reminded her of a news story that had been circulating. Someone with the unique skill to manipulate monsters had gone missing inside a dungeon. "The story all over the news. You...!" she cried.

"You heard of my exploits? I'm honored! Yes, I was the killer and I claimed that skill."

He'd killed Katagiri right in front of her, and he admitted to another murder. After all of this evidence, she couldn't deny the truth.

"I manipulated these monsters because I wanted to see your skill in action. You know, if a student dies during one of these training exercises, the odds of the Dungeon Association canceling them are pretty high. This might be my only chance to steal from a student, but your skill is oh so worth it. Thank you for your cooperation, Amane Hana."

Like a serpent, his mouth split into a grin. "Enough preamble. Time to clean up."

The system suddenly spoke inside her head.

"Oh—?!"

"*You have been chosen as the Plunderer's target.*"

"*This decision cannot be rescinded unless the target and the activator agree.*"

She was doomed. He'd chosen her as his prey, and there was no going back.

"Target set," he taunted. "I do have to touch my chosen target, but when you touched *me* to activate Stock, that condition was fulfilled. Now, shall we get on with things?"

Leisurely, Yanagi ambled toward her. If she didn't escape, he would kill her for sure. Hana spun and dashed away on trembling legs.

Whoa! she thought as she careened forward. She could run much faster than she expected. *That's right! I leveled up!*

Defeating the treants raised her level significantly. As much as she disliked using a borrowed skill to beat them, she couldn't hate it anymore. Her top priority was to get out of the dungeon.

Sadly, it wouldn't be that easy.

"Oh, no, you don't. Treant, catch her!" he shouted.

The treant launched countless branches and vines at her. She was a sitting duck—*wait*. She had one last option!

"Bullet!" she cried, hands outstretched. That black mana launched from her hands, exploded the branches and vines, and sent the treant's body tumbling. Yanagi drooped and raised his hands in disbelief at the sight.

"What in the world? I thought you drained your MP—wait, no. You used the MP you gained from leveling up, didn't you?"

Now's my chance!

While Yanagi was occupied, Hana sprinted off again.

"Oh, where do you think you're going?" he called after her. In a flash, he slid in front of her and blocked her path.

She skidded to a halt. "How?!"

One deft kick from him sent her crashing to the ground. Pain unlike anything she'd ever felt flared inside her, but it didn't incapacitate her. Not yet. She willed her newly stat-boosted body to keep fighting.

In the corner of her vision, she noticed her HP bar had fallen to half.

One more kick and I'm done for?

Chills crawled like spiders down her back, paralyzing her. Yanagi smirked down at her.

"*Oho.* You endured that hit? Your level rose higher than I expected." He hummed, clearly enjoying himself. "Might as well test *this* out."

A large ball of fire swirled out of the air into his upturned palm. The heat flickered across Hana's skin even from a distance.

"This fire magic comes from the LV 9 Advanced Magic skill I stole from Katagiri," he monologued. "I think it'll be overkill, *pardon* the expression, but I'm excited to see what it does to you!"

He sounded certain that he could end her life in one strike. He wasn't even looking at her anymore, consumed in his own world as he stared into the fire.

In her head, hazy as it was with pain, Hana knew the truth: Yanagi was about to kill her. There was nothing she could do to stop him.

I don't want this...!

As much as her mind understood the fate that awaited her, her heart rebelled inside the cage of her chest. Wasn't there some kind of hope? Until this day, she had lived a safe and comfortable life. She'd never felt the shadow of death pass anywhere near her. Now, it was cast directly over her, blocking out all but the faintest light.

Years of her life—years of *memories*—rose up in her mind's eye.

She may not know death, but she knew loss. When she was younger, her mother and father went missing in a plane crash overseas. The cause was a monster attack. After a dungeon collapse on an uninhabited island, the monsters had escaped and wreaked havoc. Something forced the plane to crash-land on the island, a place where no adventurers could protect the passengers. Everyone inside the plane went missing.

Hana wasn't so young that she failed to understand *missing* meant *presumed dead*. Old enough to understand they were gone, but not old enough to control her emotions. The sudden weight of loss left her crying for what felt like forever.

And her brother, Amane Rin, was her rock in the midst of a wicked storm.

He always held her hand and remained by her side. Thanks to him, she found she could rise again, no matter how many times she fell. She was beyond grateful, and she made sure he knew it. She only had one regret.

Did oniichan...ever cry?

As she drifted through her memories, she saw him again and again, strong and secure. Not once had she seen him cry. Her heart swelled with sorrow. She wondered if he thought he couldn't cry in front of her. Had she robbed him of his chance to properly grieve?

"I'm sorry," she sobbed. "I'm sorry, oniichan."

Her guilt would never reach him, but she had to say it. Tears overflowed from her eyes and pooled on the ground. Her cries bounced off the cold walls of the dungeon.

"Ah..."

Through her tears, she saw her red ribbon had fallen near her hand. It had come untied when Yanagi kicked her away.

An uneasy feeling overtook her, as if she'd forgotten something very important. She reached for the ribbon as if to reach that memory. Once her fingertips found the ribbon, it rushed back.

Months after their parents were declared missing, Hana still found herself crying in her room alone every day. Time and time again, Rin was there to help her find her footing, but she often slipped back into grief.

One day, she found the strength to leave her room and go to *him* in the living room.

"Oniichan...good morning," she managed.

"...Yeah. Morning, Hana."

He blinked at seeing her there, but quickly smiled.

"Listen, Oniichan. I need to tell you something—"

"Come here, Hana," he interrupted.

"Huh? All right..."

She dried her tears and sat in front of him. He pulled a red ribbon from somewhere and used it to tie back her hair.

"What're you doing?" she asked.

"Your hair grew out, can't you tell? This is a present for you. There, all done."

He handed a mirror to her, which she used to see her new ponytail. It was an unusual hairstyle on her.

"It's...kinda messy," she said.

"Oof. Tough critic. Want to tie it back yourself?"

"No, I'll leave it. I like it."

"Okay."

They fell silent for a short while. Hana appreciated he'd thought of her, but that was why she knew she had to speak.

"Listen, oniichan—" she began. She wanted to apologize for the burden she'd been. Before she could speak, Rin placed his hand on her head.

"Don't worry," he said. "You don't need to say anything else."

"But I keep letting you support *me*. I want to help *you* too."

"It's fine, really. Big brothers are supposed to protect their sisters. I want you to know that." He knelt in front of her so that he matched her eye level and smiled. "I'd never resent you for relying on me, so don't stop doing it, all right? If you're ever hurting or sad, I'll protect you. If I'm not strong enough to help, I'll get stronger until I am."

In that moment, Hana understood why Rin didn't want her to apologize. He didn't *need* her to.

"Thanks, oniichan."

"Of course."

Finally, Hana brought herself to smile alongside him.

I remember.

How had she forgotten? Rin would never expect her to say sorry. She'd only tried to apologize to relieve her own guilt.

There's something else I have to do!

She remembered what Rin had told her. *If you're ever hurting or sad, I'll protect you. If I'm not strong enough to help, I'll get stronger until I am,* he'd said.

Once Rin became an adventurer and was told he had no talent for it, no matter how weak he was, he worked himself to the bone to gain what he could. But there were limits to what was possible. Yanagi was probably stronger than he was, to the point where even if she asked for Rin's help, he had no chance of winning.

Could she still depend on him despite that?

There was no more time to wonder. Yanagi pulled his eyes away from the swirl of the fireball and declared, "Let's put an end to this."

"Go," he commanded the giant fireball. It launched toward her.

It undoubtedly contained the power to end her life. She had no hope of dodging or surviving the attack. Those facts drove her to a decision: even if it was pointless, she would struggle until the last millisecond. She knew he wouldn't—*couldn't*—come to her aid, but with every ounce of effort she had left, she closed her eyes and screamed.

"Help me, oniichan!!!"

Her scream rang out through the dungeon, but the only sound that echoed back to her ears was her own voice. She hadn't expected a response, and yet, in her heart—

"Leave it to me," Rin said.

No way...!

In the inky dark behind her eyelids, she *knew* she heard his voice. Slowly, she opened her eyes. Somehow, the fireball had disappeared, supplanted by the steady back of the person she wanted to see more than anyone. He gripped a crimson blade in one hand.

"Oniichan!"

Rin turned around and nodded with a comforting smile. He moved closer and took a knee before her. The short sword he held vanished into some sort of space she couldn't see. She hugged him with all her might.

"You...you really came!" she cried.

"Of course I did. That's what big brothers are for," he replied kindly. He withdrew a liquid-filled bottle from that invisible space. "This is a health recovery potion. Drink it."

"Mm! I will!"

She drank it, and he placed his hand gently on her head.

"You did great, Hana. You're safe now. Leave the rest to me."

"O-okay!"

Hearing his words made relief wash over her, like she was already saved. Yanagi eyed the two of them dubiously.

"How are you even here?" he asked sharply. "And why didn't you take any damage from that magic attack? Answer me, Amane Rin!"

Rin rose slowly, his back still turned to Yanagi. "Before that, answer a question for me. Did you try to kill Hana?"

"...You know what? I did. I'm going to kill her and steal her unique skill because I have the power to do that. *Satisfied?*" Yanagi sneered.

"Yes. I understand perfectly now," Rin replied evenly.

He slowly faced Yanagi. Unlike when Rin faced Hana, rage was plainly scrawled in angry strokes across his face. He moved to close the distance between them.

"Oh, what? I answered you honestly, and you're not going to answer *my* question?" Yanagi said. "*Whatever*. I've got an answer for you. Get up, treant!"

"How—" Hana began, but the sight before her stole her words. The treant she thought she'd destroyed repaired its body and rose again.

Horrified, she remembered that the system hadn't said anything about leveling up when it fell. Her attack wasn't strong enough, so the treant survived and bided its time.

"Kill him!" Yanagi shouted.

The treant obeyed, launching its large body at Rin with astonishing speed, its branches and vines twining into a club that it swung at him.

"Oniichan, watch out!" she screamed.

She had no idea how Rin blocked the fire magic, but considering his level, he wasn't strong enough to defeat the treant. For a second, she regretted calling out for him. Asking for his help led to this. She had put them both in danger.

In the next second, she witnessed something unbelievable.

Rin's blade met the treant's attack head on.

"You're in my way," he said in an ice-cold voice. His arm *blurred* as he slashed. The treant's thick wooden body splintered and exploded like a balloon popped by a sharp needle.

"...What?" she gasped.

"The hell?" Yanagi snarled.

Hana and Yanagi, the only witnesses to the miracle, reacted with shock. Meanwhile, Rin wore a neutral expression, as if this amount of power was natural to him.

He turned to Yanagi and said coolly, "I *will* take you down."

Deep darkness glinted in Rin's eyes.

CHAPTER 6

PLUNDERER

EARLIER, inside the Remote Magic Tower.

"...What's going on?" Rin asked. His eyes widened at the hologram in front of him. It showed a large treelike monster and a young man—Yanagi, he recognized after a moment—fighting it. A shaking girl stood in the corner of the image, watching the fight.

"Hana!" Rin gasped.

His heart leapt into his throat. There was clearly a problem. What in the world had happened? Questions crowded and clouded his mind, but he tried to stay calm and make sense of the situation. He had no idea how this image was connected to dungeons on a foundational level. The system said it deemed this information the most valuable to him. What information was it trying to convey?

"Is it showing me something that's happening right now?"

He'd lost track of exactly how many days he'd been inside the Remote Magic Tower, but if memory served, today *was* the day of Hana's dungeon practice. Did that mean this image was part of it? He studied it closely.

"That shouldn't be possible. Such a high-level monster wouldn't spawn inside an E-rank dungeon, and Hana would never be left alone with Yanagi-san. Something isn't right..."

Regardless of how the situation had started, if he didn't go to her, her life could be in danger. Yanagi was fighting on par with the monster, but the balance could easily tip. Someone had to save them before the monster killed Yanagi.

Just then, Rin's thoughts hitched, and he felt as if something important had slipped out of his hands. He faltered for a moment, but instinct demanded he rush to the scene immediately. He didn't have time to catch a stray thought.

"Hey, system! Get me out of here!" Rin hollered at the top of his lungs.

"Challenger's intentions confirmed. Now exiting the Remote Magic Tower."

A soft glow surrounded his body and lifted him from the ground. The teleportation spell deposited him outside, leaving the tower soaring in front of him, any remaining secrets locked inside.

He sensed some sort of *intention*—something he hadn't sensed before beating the tower. What *was* this dungeon? What was that third prize? Why did it give him an image as a consolation prize? He didn't like leaving without knowing the truth, but he didn't have time to mull it over.

"It's forbidden to use skills outside a dungeon, but I won't get something for nothing," he reasoned to himself. "She's at Sumifuku, right? Evasion will get me out of here."

Rin took off running. Just then, he thought he heard a voice. Something nostalgic.

"You can do it, Rin."

Did oniichan really come here? But how?

Hana watched Rin take down the treant in one strike, staring in unbridled amazement. She hadn't even seen him enter the room, and such powerful attacks were beyond his abilities.

Wait—maybe they're not!

He'd let her copy his Conceal skill to hide Stock from prying eyes. When she asked why he knew a skill like that, he put off answering her. Seeing him, she could guess why. He wanted to hide his true abilities and used Conceal to do it. *Was* there a reason for him to hide it? Hana wasn't sure.

Yanagi let out a belly laugh, completely unconcerned that the monster he'd manipulated was obliterated. He quivered with glee, not fear, as he spoke to Rin.

"I'm surprised, Amane Rin. I didn't expect you to defeat a treant in one strike," he said. "You're only level 5,000."

Rin's brow furrowed. "Did I say that was my level?"

"Oh, are you surprised to hear that I discovered your *real* level?" Yanagi taunted. "My unique skill, Plunderer, lets me see the level of anyone I touch. Does that ring any bells in your little head?"

"...We shook hands when we met."

"That's right. I instantly saw you were hiding your true power, and there's only one reason for that! You have a skill you can't tell anyone about, don't you?"

Rin kept his mouth shut, but the silence spoke for itself. He might as well have said yes.

"I decided right then and there that I wanted your skill all to myself! I was disappointed to hear you wouldn't be joining us today, so imagine my surprise when you showed up on your own! I can plunder your sister's skill *and* yours in one go! Lucky, lucky *me*!" His grin widened, stressing the corners of his mouth. "That said, I can't have you get in the way of your sister's murder. I'll pick you off first."

The system intruded on Hana's mind.

"Plunderer wishes to change the target. Do you consent?"

"What?!" she yelped.

"You heard it, right?" Yanagi asked. "Sorry to bother you, but I can only target one person at a time, so I'm changing it from you to him. *Please* hurry up and agree."

"I would never!"

She suspected he needed to switch the target or he wouldn't gain the skill from killing Rin first. If she consented, she'd hand him the exact conditions he wanted to fulfill his plan. She turned to Rin, her brows knitted together.

"Give your consent, Hana," Rin said.

"W-what? But you'll—"

"Don't worry. Trust me," he said confidently. She knew her brother must have an idea, so Hana nodded. There was no one she trusted more.

"Okay. I...I consent."

The system confirmed that she was no longer a target. She was left with stillness in her mind as the system switched to Rin.

"You have been chosen as the Plunderer's target."

"This decision cannot be rescinded unless the target and the activator agree."

"So, that's how it works," Rin said to himself.

This makes the fight a whole lot easier.

Yanagi was dead set on stealing his and Hana's skills. He wouldn't have a reason to go after her when Rin was the active target. Rin worried Yanagi might take Hana hostage, but this lowered the chance, since Yanagi needed her alive to get Stock.

All Rin had to do was defeat him. He stepped forward.

Yanagi grinned.

"Ah, familial love. You idiots," he mocked. "If you had the balls to ditch your sister, you could've saved yourself. You think you can beat me?"

Rin didn't answer.

"You got a big head from defeating a weakened treant, so I'll teach you a lesson. It's impossible for a worm like you to defeat me!"

To Rin's amazement, seven giant monsters materialized around Yanagi. Appraisal revealed they had names like orc king, salamander, king ice wolf, and even more level-10,000 monsters. A daunting roster.

"How did you do that…?" Rin muttered.

"The same thing I did to the treants. I can use my plundered Tamer skill to recruit any monster lower level than I am to fight for me!"

Rin narrowed his eyes. "Their levels are higher than yours."

"Kid, you're not the sharpest tool in the shed, are you? I pulled the same trick you did."

"…Conceal."

Yanagi's lips curled. "Exactly. My real level is over 10,000, and I have more powerful plundered skills than your thick head can imagine. My abilities vastly outweigh adventurers of a similar level! There's no way you're getting out of here alive!" he spat.

Yanagi lifted his hand and a jagged spike of lightning crackled overhead. As if it was their signal, the monsters positioned themselves for battle. With militaristic precision, the ones that specialized in close combat formed the front line, while the magic users prepared to support from the rear. They all turned to face Rin.

"I've been dreaming of it, but now I'll kill you for real," Yanagi cackled like the arrogant villain he was, as if the battle was already won. "I don't know what tricks you have up your sleeve, but don't think you can wriggle out of this! *Now die, Amane Rin!*"

Yanagi's signal prompted his force to attack in unison. The magic attacks hit Rin first. Lightning struck and rocked the ground. Flames raced forward, fervent enough to melt metal. Spears of ice stabbed from the sky. Each was a direct attack, just for him.

Hana lay behind him, so he couldn't afford to dodge. Even if he could, the orc king and the other close-combat monsters surged at him in a wave, ready to strike. He was trapped with no hope and no way out. The epitome of despair.

"Come on, Nameless," he said in a steady voice.

Light gleamed from the white metal of the longsword in his right hand. A crimson short sword manifested in his left. He stepped forward as if the path ahead of him was as clear and serene as a cool spring evening.

Despair had no hold on him.

Now die, Amane Rin!

A bevy of magic attacks—each strong enough to kill a level-10,000 adventurer easily—descended upon Rin. Yanagi knew he was victorious. No matter how confident, Rin couldn't withstand an attack like that.

The sight of the magic dissipating in an instant stopped him in his tracks.

"How the hell?!" he shrieked.

Rin emerged from the magic without a scratch on him. It was impossible, yet there he was. No level-5,000 adventurer could survive that vicious of a barrage! But Yanagi didn't have time to panic. Rin was sprinting toward him at extraordinary speed.

"Oh, no, you *don't*!" Yanagi said, collecting himself. "Stop him!" he commanded his monsters.

He had to think. Rin clearly had some kind of magic resistant technique. Odds were, *that* was his special skill. If that was the case, how would he handle a direct physical attack? Out of his tamed monsters, the orc king had the highest raw strength.

"Crush him, orc king!"

The orc king roared and smashed his giant iron axe onto Rin. No way would Rin block that! Yanagi was positive, but Rin defied him once again.

"Too late," he said.

"What?!"

Rin was faster now, somehow. He swung his sword so rapidly that all Yanagi saw was the flash the blade left behind. The king orc's body hit the ground in two pieces. Yanagi gawked, but the assault didn't stop there. Rin's relentless silver sword obliterated the *entire force* of level-10,000 monsters.

"What *are* you?!" Yanagi groaned. No answer came. Only Rin did—he stopped right in front of him. Yanagi threw himself away from the swipe of his sword.

For Yanagi, a specialist in speed, to dodge so narrowly meant that Rin's speed was completely unreasonable. He couldn't let his guard down. If he did, Rin would rush him for sure! Yanagi took a defensive stance, but Rin didn't close the distance between them. Instead, he turned the now-four-colored short sword in his left hand toward Yanagi. The blade glowed with light: crimson, rose, azure, and gold.

Rin said, "Release."

The short sword expelled a massive ball of flame, much like the one Yanagi had launched at him.

"Ngh!" he grunted as he dodged the surprise attack, just barely. It grazed his left shoulder, leaving behind a burn. He gripped it with his right hand and glared at Rin. One of the colors that shone on his short sword had disappeared. Yanagi reached out and grasped the truth.

"I get it!" he said. "You..."

With the information Rin had revealed so far, the pieces slotted together. Considering the magic attacks hadn't scratched him, the short sword releasing fire magic explained everything.

Amane Hana could harmlessly borrow skills from people with Stock.

Yanagi Souji had to kill people to steal their skills.

Amane Rin's short sword could steal magic before it killed *him*.

One thing was clear.

"That's a plunderer sword!" he accused.

Rin didn't answer. He raised the three-colored short sword. "Here we go, Greed," he told it, then looked at Yanagi and said, "You can have these back."

A plunderer versus a plunderer's sword. It would be a duel to the death.

MAGIC-STEALING SHORT SWORD, GREED
A reward given to those who defeat the Remote Magic Tower.
RECOMMENDED EQUIP LEVEL: 13,000
ATTACK +60%

When magic strikes this blade, the wielder may pay MP equivalent to the cost to cast the magic and absorb it. The absorbed magic may be activated at no cost.

STORAGE CAPACITY: Maximum seven types of magic.

CHAPTER 7

ZERO

JUST BEFORE RIN first attacked Yanagi, he noticed something. He didn't sense Nameless's effects activate, which indicated Yanagi's level hovered somewhere between ten thousand and thirteen thousand. That Yanagi could dodge Rin, a speed-focused adventurer himself, denoted some serious dexterity stats. Add to that Yanagi's use of daggers, a weapon favored by the speedy. With such clear evidence, Rin decided Nameless wasn't the best weapon for their fight.

"Switch," he commanded his Item Box. Speed Sword swapped places with Nameless in his right hand.

SPEED SWORD

A short sword made with a Blacksmith skill.

RECOMMENDED EQUIP LEVEL: 6,000

ATTACK +6,000

SPEED +3,000

Attack power was unlikely to determine the outcome of this fight. Rather, speed would. Thus, Rin decided to dual-wield Greed and his Speed Sword. Ready to fight, he lunged after Yanagi.

Yanagi clicked his tongue in frustration, fully focused on Rin's short swords. Against the slashing short swords, he could barely defend himself.

He's fast, Yanagi thought. *And each attack is so heavy! What's with this guy?!*

As the two traded blows, Yanagi felt that Rin's physical strength was higher than his own. Doubts arose in his mind, much like the way the ache from blocking Rin's blows crept up his arm.

Impossible, impossible, impossible!!! He was only level 5,000 a few days ago! Does his unique skill multiply his strength this much? How else would he have gotten so strong in such a short time?!

Even for Yanagi, who took pride in his rapid leveling, leveling up so much was outside the realm of possibility. His whole being rejected the notion that the levels Rin seemed to have gained were real.

Obviously, he wasn't going to ask Rin how he did it. At this rate, he would lose. He had to think of something—a different method to turn the tides!

Yanagi had stolen many fantastic skills with Plunderer, so one of them should've come to mind, but his vision was clouded by the flash of Rin's tri-colored sword.

"I hate it!" he yelled childishly. "If it weren't for that annoying short sword!"

Tallying the skills he'd plundered, he found that half of them were magic. Each one of them boasted the power to reverse the situation, but as long as Rin wielded that short sword, Yanagi's magic would be turned back on *him*.

The more he gnawed on the problem, the larger it felt. The short sword must have activation limits, but he couldn't test his theories. It was all he could do to evade Rin's attacks and block his blades. Yanagi's only saving grace was the difference in raw stats, which allowed him to focus on defense. At least, as long as he didn't use magic, Rin wouldn't have magic to steal.

There would be an opening and chance to counterattack *somewhere*, but he couldn't skate on thin ice forever.

"Release," Rin commanded.

"No!!!"

Rin slashed his blade. Yanagi panicked, and his response to the action was too late. Greed released a spear of ice that pierced his right foot and pinned him in place.

"Ghhh!" he choked out.

Rin didn't hesitate to swing Speed Sword at him.

Not like this! Yanagi thought. He wasn't meek prey. He couldn't dodge anymore, but he could block! He raised his dagger in front of his chest, barely—but successfully—saving himself.

The short swords in Rin's hands vanished. "Wise Man," he said.

"Huh?"

As Rin said the strange words, he punched Yanagi solidly in the chest. He heaved as each fist pummeled his ribs and sent him flying. Faster than he could see, he struck a wall, back first. Thorny, strangling agony lanced through his body. White sparks framed his vision as his HP fell by nearly 30 percent.

What did he...he punched me bare-handed? That power doesn't make any sense for bare hands! Who is he?!

He pressed his left hand to his chest and desperately turned his head. Rin ran toward Yanagi faster than his thoughts could race. The short swords were back in Rin's hands. Yanagi couldn't move, let alone run.

Is this my end? he agonized.

If Rin struck him a few more times, he was bound to die. Facing death might've made someone else's life slow down as it flashed before their eyes, but his thoughts picked up speed.

I'm going to lose to a guy like him?

As if that was possible.

I'm going to be stolen from again?

As if he would allow that to happen.

If it means survival...I'll bet my life!

"One-winged Flight," he said.

He would play the last card in his deck.

ONE-WINGED FLIGHT LV 6
+60% to Speed (Decreases HP by 1% per second).

One-winged Flight had more negatives than positives, so it was a skill that disgusted Yanagi to his very core. Gale Wind, which anyone could obtain, didn't have such a dangerous price attached to it. With his HP already low, he didn't want to rely on it—but in the face of death, he was out of options. This useless skill was the only way to overcome Rin's LV 10 Gale Wind.

Even if I have to gamble everything...

"I'll kill you, Amane Rin!" He swallowed the pain and ran toward him. "Take this!"

"Huh?!" Rin gasped.

One-winged Flight propelled his speed beyond Rin's by far. He couldn't elude Yanagi any longer.

I can do this!

Yanagi slashed Rin's side with invisible speed, far faster than he could dodge. The high of success flooded him—until a *ting* sound vibrated up his blade.

"Why are you *like* this?!" he screamed in fury.

No matter how tough Rin was, it was impossible for a human body to make that high-pitched sound. Somehow, an invisible barrier surrounded Rin. Yanagi had put everything he had behind that attack, but it was deflected like *nothing*.

Oh, but he wasn't going to cry and beg for mercy so submissively! His mind was made up.

"Well, color me surprised, Amane Rin," he drawled. "You have a defense against physical attacks too. How funny! Allow me to see *how long it lasts*!"

Yanagi refused to stop until his HP drained to zero. He ran circles around Rin and struck pitilessly with his daggers. This time, he was on offense, and Rin was on defense, but he couldn't match Yanagi's speed fast enough to block. Even though Rin could follow Yanagi's movements with his eyes, he couldn't keep up.

With Rin unable to evade or defend, Yanagi showered him in slash attacks until the moment he'd waited for arrived. One powerful strike at Rin's back resulted in a cracking sound, as if something glass-fragile had broken.

"I knew there was a limit!" Yanagi gloated. "I'll break it entirely next time!"

"Release," Rin whispered.

A ball of fire shot from Greed. Yanagi sidestepped it by a millisecond. He didn't appreciate the interruption in his string of attacks, but Rin only had one more spell to wield, making one less thing for Yanagi to worry about. *One more strike!*

Yanagi flew faster than he ever had before.

"Time to die, Amane Rin!"

Rin faced Yanagi head on and stilled. Was Rin just a rabbit, frozen under the shadow of a swooping hawk? Or was he baiting Yanagi into letting his guard down?

You freakin' idiot. I know you're strong in your own right, but that's exactly why I'll do everything it takes to kill you!

Still...something was off.

Why isn't he afraid?

Rin's eyes flashed defiantly, almost as if he didn't believe death was imminent.

I'm imagining it. My victory is secure! This strike will end him!

He swung his dagger wide. No matter how much Rin's stats had multiplied, he wasn't fast enough to evade him.

At least, that was what he believed. He had no idea what his prey was truly capable of.

If Yanagi had made just one mistake, it was this: he'd acted without knowing what Rin's unique skill could do—and without knowing that it *no longer required activation time.*

"Dungeon Teleportation, LV 20," Rin whispered. "Time Zero."

Yanagi had been outrun.

Rin slashed his two short swords and abused his teleportation to rapidly strike at Yanagi. He defended himself—if it could be called defense. It would be more accurate to say he was overwhelmed. Rin struck his back, sides, legs, and shoulders with his swords.

Amidst the assault, Yanagi hissed at him, "Instant chain teleportation! Speed that disregards *speed* itself and elevates your swordsmanship to godly realms! Admit it, *that's* your power, Amane Rin!"

If used creatively, it could be one of the most phenomenal abilities out there. Faced with a power like this, Yanagi felt speed—his one advantage—slip like sand through his fingers. There was only one thing he could do against Rin's attacks. He used Enemy Detection to nail down Rin's position and avoid lethal blows in the fractions of a second that they came. But the more he avoided them, the more stamina he lost. His HP had already fallen below 50 percent, and One-winged Flight drained it further, drip by drip.

He'll beat me at this rate! I have to find a moment to counterattack, but then—! Yanagi glared at the yellow gleam on the short sword in Rin's left hand. *I need to consider his counterattack. He can strike with magic on top of regular sword attacks, and I doubt I can handle that. If I could just get him to waste that magic!*

He desperately searched for an idea, but he didn't have time to settle on one. His step snagged on the ground and dragged his rapid speed to a near halt.

"*Rghhh!*"

In a fight of this level, sloppy mistakes could cost his life. Rin wouldn't let this opening get away.

Short swords tight in his hands, Rin rushed Yanagi head on. His intent was clear; this was the finale. No reason to teleport, no reason to evade. Yanagi raised his daggers in a defensive stand, intending to block, but Rin suddenly changed tactics.

"Release."

"H-huh?!"

Yanagi was prepared to absorb a melee strike. At this close range, the spell would engulf him.

Candescent lightning crackled above him. It was impossible to dodge—or was it? In what should have been a moment of disaster, Yanagi smirked.

"You fell for it!"

Surprise flashed across Rin's face. Yanagi bent with remarkable speed and slipped under the lightning by the skin of his teeth. Everything from his stumble to defending was a trap to lure Rin into wasting his last magic attack. Yanagi used that momentum to race toward him.

But Rin wasn't so easily caught without a plan.

"Time Zero," he said, vanishing from sight.

Enemy Detection revealed his location to Yanagi. Behind him!

"You're a one-trick pony!" Yanagi snarled. He'd anticipated this too. Everything about Rin's attacks telegraphed he would teleport into Yanagi's blind spot once again. Knowing that, he reacted in time.

He whirled around and struck out with his dagger. There was no way Rin could counter that!

He swiped at the air.

"What?"

Rin was two meters away, just out of reach of his blade. His short sword pointed at Yanagi, still gleaming yellow.

"Release."

Lightning flashed and struck Yanagi head on. He screamed as every nerve in his body convulsed with heat and light. The smell of burning filled the air as his HP fell below 20 percent.

What was that, what happened?! I dodged that magic! Didn't he waste the spell? Don't tell me—?!

An unfathomable thought came to him. There was no other explanation.

Did he use teleportation to reabsorb his magic attack?!

A magic-stealing sword and teleportation magic: those two powers made an impossible fighting style possible. Rin was living proof.

He's a monster!

Yanagi saw the writing on the wall. Rin's strength, weapons, skills, and ingenuity surpassed his own. Rin's next attack *would* end everything. Yanagi had thrown everything he had at Rin, but nothing stuck.

I'll admit it, Amane Rin. You're stronger than I am. But you've forgotten one key detail!

Yanagi flung the dagger in his left hand with as much power as he could muster. It swiped past Rin without fanfare, but that was fine. He wasn't aiming for him.

Amane Hana shrieked as the dagger sailed toward her. Until that moment, Rin had been level-headed, but Hana's scream spurred him to move with panic. Yanagi regarded them with scorn.

You might be stronger than me, but only in battle. I'm a survivor, and survivors win. Sorry, but victory is mine!

Forget obtaining Stock from Hana: killing Rin was his priority. Once he was no longer targeting her, honestly, he didn't care about killing her. She wasn't the target of Plunderer. Besides, since Rin had taken his bait, the odds of Hana dying before him were suddenly *much* lower.

You wouldn't let your precious sister die, would you, Amane Rin?! You'll use teleportation and your short sword to protect her! Your stupid sappy sibling bond will open you up to a decisive killing blow!

Predictably, Rin said, "Time Zero."

As he expected, Rin cared more about defending Hana than attacking him.

Now!

Knowing this was it, Yanagi sprinted—and choked on shock when Rin cut him off.

Why did he teleport in front of me, not the dagger?! He abandoned his sister?!

He couldn't understand Rin's actions, and with Rin in his path, he stretched to see Hana—

Clang!

The hard sound marked the dagger deflecting off Hana's body.

Is his sister cloaked in the same barrier?!

The invisible barrier around Rin's body that nullified Yanagi's blows...he never imagined Rin could activate it around Hana. When Yanagi threw his dagger, Rin made an expression of alarm. That was a ploy. Rin had fooled *him* in return.

The racing of Yanagi's thoughts halted. He was drained. None of this—he predicted *none* of this.

Rin faced Yanagi with stone-cold eyes. These were surely his final moments.

In an instant, Rin was right in front of Yanagi.

"Amane Rin...!" he barked, like it was a curse. His face was twisted with desperation as he swung at Rin.

"You made the wrong choice," Rin said.

"What?!"

Rin deflected Yanagi's dagger strike with the Speed Sword in his left hand. Yanagi lost his grip and his second dagger skittered across the floor.

Rage, hatred, bloodlust—Rin suppressed all of it and spoke with an even voice. "You put your hands on someone you *never* should have touched."

In the back of his mind, Yanagi remembered Hana's warm smile.

Rin drew his left hand—the one holding Greed—back like a bow and arrow. He poured the spiteful emotions in his chest into that one movement. Just like the magic, it seemed as though Greed devoured them.

"Some choices are *unforgiveable*!"

Rin released his fury. Yanagi tried to escape, but he was far too slow. A torrent of blows rained down on him faster than the speed of sound. One stab that could rend the heavens sank deep, deep into Yanagi's heart.

He gasped.

Rin withdrew the sword.

Yanagi slowly slumped to the ground. He coughed, blood leaking from his mouth, with the expression of a man who knew his life was over.

Rin looked down at him, Greed tight in his hand, and said, "I win."

The curtain closed on their performance, and Amane Rin was the only one left standing.

Everything was hazy.

Like a puppet with cut strings, Yanagi's head hung down. He watched the blood leak from his chest.

Oh. I lost...

He couldn't move a finger. Yes, he would certainly die right here and now, and nothing could change that simple fact. Amane

Rin, the one who stabbed him in the heart—a boy, just a *boy*—watched him with unfeeling eyes.

I never expected he'd best me this thoroughly. An ugly, wet laugh wracked his chest. *In the end, I was the one in the palm of his hand.*

A magic-stealing sword, invisible barriers, and teleportation. Rin had used so many tricks to destroy his plan, corner him, and run his heart through. After all his villainous talk crumbled to nothing, Yanagi only had one question left.

"Tell me...Amane Rin," he croaked. "Have you...killed someone before?"

Rin regarded him silently for a moment.

"No. This'll be my first time taking a life."

"...Then you're a real *monster*."

He had to be. To not flinch in the face of the bloodlust turned his way; to take that bloodlust and turn it right back on his attacker without hesitation. That spoke to who he was.

As for Yanagi...

The first time he killed someone, his hand trembled as he gripped the knife. He ran from the truth—that even though his actions were in self-defense, he had stolen a life. That younger version of himself couldn't face his victim, the way Rin did now. Had he ever faced it?

Maybe the result of this battle was decided from the start.

His consciousness slipped, and he mustered his final words to Rin.

"I'll keep an eye on you to see how you use that power..."

Yanagi's breaths stopped. There was quiet.

◆ ⌃ ◆

Yanagi stopped breathing before my eyes. At the same time, the system spoke in my mind.

"Gained XP: Level increased by 121!"

"Obtained skill: Plunderer."

"Plunderer has been reset to LV 1."

The words stunned me. "I obtained Plunderer...?"

As startled as I was, part of me understood. Plunderer required permission from the target to switch to someone else. I surmised there was a hidden reason for the target to have a say in the matter, though I hadn't imagined winning the skill was it.

That explained Yanagi's final words. He knew the Plunderer ability would transfer to me. He *knew*. Did that mean...

Could he have stolen this skill from someone *he* killed?

I turned on my heel, away from his corpse. Even though he was gone, I swore to him anyway.

"Even with the same power, I'll never turn into someone like *you*."

Those words bounced off the walls and faded into the distance.

AMANE RIN

LEVEL: 13,617

SP: 8,710

TITLES: Dungeon Traveler (10/10), Nameless Swordsman, Endbringer (ERROR), Wiser Wise Man

HP: 39,280/106,680   MP: 3,680/29,490

ATTACK: 25,450   DEFENSE: 21,480   SPEED: 26,620

INTELLIGENCE: 21,160   RESISTANCE: 21,240   LUCK: 20,220

SKILLS: Dungeon Teleportation LV 20, Enhanced Strength LV MAX,
   Herculean Strength LV MAX, Superhuman Strength LV MAX,
   High-speed Movement LV MAX, Gale Wind LV MAX,
   Revitalize LV 1, Purification Magic LV 1, Mana Boost LV MAX,
   Mana Recovery LV 2, Enemy Detection LV 4, Evasion LV 4,
   Status Condition Resistance LV 4, Appraisal, Item Box LV 5,
   Conceal LV 1, Battle Barrier LV 1, Plunderer LV 1

DUNGEON TELEPORTATION LV 20

REQUIRED MP: 1 MP × distance (meters)

CONDITIONS: Teleportation can only occur in dungeons that have
   already been visited.

TELEPORTATION DISTANCE: Maximum 400 meters.

ACTIVATION TIME: 0.8 seconds × distance (meters)

SCOPE: User and user's belongings.

SUB-SKILL: TIME ZERO

Paying 100 MP allows the user to teleport instantly within a
   ten-meter radius. (This ability is obtained when Dungeon
   Teleportation reaches LV 20).

PLUNDERER LV 1

CONDITIONS: Killing the target allows the user to steal one of their skills. If a skill is not chosen, this ability will steal the target's highest-level skill. If the user is killed by the target, this skill transfers to the target and is reset to LV 1. Targets must be touched directly.

PLUNDERING CAPACITY: 1 type.

As I walked away from Yanagi's body, I checked my stats display. It showed, *MP: 3,680/29,490.*

"I may have come out on top, but that was a close one," I said to myself. Fortunately, I'd had two new powers at my disposal: Greed and Time Zero.

My sword, Greed, was the second reward from the Remote Magic Tower. Time Zero was the result of boosting Dungeon Teleportation's level to twenty so I could reach Sumifuku and find Hana as soon as possible. My only goal was shortening the time required to teleport as much as possible, but this new sub-skill was a *major* bonus.

Together, these two tools formed a powerful weapon, but the severe mana requirements were a downside to the combo. Greed required the same MP cost as the magic it stole, and Time Zero required 100 MP for each use. Since this was the first time I'd used the combination, it was possible there were also downsides I couldn't see yet.

I intended to practice before using the two in such a high-stakes fight, but once I tasted Yanagi's strength, I knew I couldn't hold back. That was how threatening an intelligent opponent was.

If it was just a difference in physical strength—like the lightning beast had shown me—that was one thing. But in this case, one wrong slash, one wrong judgment about who I was up against... *I* would've ended up dead.

My thoughts heavy, I walked over to Hana.

"Are you okay?" I asked, taking a knee in front of her. Relief must've hit her hard because she practically jumped on me.

"Oniichan!" she said shakily.

"Whoa, there!"

"I was *so* scared...!"

"I'm sorry. You wouldn't have faced danger if I hadn't been so late."

"That's not what I meant! You nearly died because I called you for help! *That's* why I was scared."

"Hana." I patted her head. "It's over now. I'm sorry I worried you."

"It's okay, as long as you're safe."

"Thanks," I replied. "Still, that *was* scary. Did his dagger cut you at all?"

"No, thanks to you. I'm totally fine." She giggled with nervous energy.

Just in case, I inspected her for any injuries. Like she said, she didn't appear to have any fresh cuts. The tension inside me eased.

Good thing Battle Barrier could be placed on other people too.

> **BATTLE BARRIER LV 1**
> By draining MP, this skill creates a mana barrier around the
> target. (Note: The strength and duration of the effect changes
> according to skill level.)
> **COOLDOWN TIME:** 60 seconds.

Like the skill description said, I had to choose a target. It didn't have to be *me*. The first thing I'd done when I arrived was activate it on her. Once Yanagi and I had our little chat and used up the sixty-second cooldown, I activated it on myself.

I wish I could've done more to prevent him targeting her in the first place, but until the very end, Yanagi fought with the feral craftiness of a cornered animal. I shuddered as I realized anew how difficult an opponent he really was.

"Hey, oniichan?" Hana said, breaking up my thoughts.

"Hm?"

"You're a lot stronger than I thought you were."

I winced. "Sorry for hiding that."

"You don't need to apologize. I get why you did it, because that's what I chose too. You had your reasons, didn't you?"

"Yeah. Once we get home, I'll give you the run-down."

"Good!"

There was no point in hiding it anymore, and Hana deserved the full story. I was just glad she was safe. There was no greater gift.

◆ ⌃ ◆

Before we emerged above ground, I asked Hana to wait while I sneaked out. I'd entered Sumifuku with Dungeon Tele-portation instead of using the Gate, so I needed to make sure my exit didn't draw attention. I used Conceal to suppress any detectable motion and surfaced. Predictably, adventurers at an E-rank dungeon didn't pick up on my secrets. Hana came up after me, alone.

The trainees who'd surfaced before her reacted with surprise, but they seemed relieved to see her safe. When she was asked why she'd been left behind, Hana told them the story we'd agreed upon: other monsters appeared along the way, and as she tried to flee, she was separated from the group but managed to find her way back. Everyone was satisfied with the answer. Afterward, I regrouped with Hana at the meeting point to blend in.

The only problem was that Yanagi and Katagiri never returned from the dungeon's depths.

After some time anxiously waiting, Dungeon Association staff members arrived. Seasoned adventurers dived to save them, only to bring their bodies—and a magic stone slab—back up. My heart thumped at the sight.

They gathered around the magic slab and spoke hurriedly. Their voices were too low for the students to hear, but my senses were sharp enough to hear clearly.

"Are the words written here true?" one asked. "Yanagi-kun killed Katagiri-san?"

"I can't believe it. He didn't seem the kind of young man capable of *murder*..."

"We need to investigate whether he truly possessed this 'Plunderer' skill. If he used it to steal Tamer, it would explain that adventurer's death."

"We can't draw any conclusions just yet, but the missing adventurer *did* have the Tamer skill. Let's go over the circumstances of his death one more time. That may clarify things."

"Agreed."

I left that slab for them to find. It described everything that happened, but I left out my and Hana's involvement.

I wasn't ready to share my true strength yet. The world wasn't ready for Dungeon Teleportation. If they found out a supposed weakling like me had the power to defeat Yanagi, the odds of me facing serious scrutiny—or worse, *tests*—would be high. It was best to stay silent about my involvement.

I made one compromise. Yanagi had used his position as a Dungeon Association member to steal many lives. I couldn't stomach concealing that awful truth, so I carved the message using one of my swords into the magic slab, like a clue left in blood by a murder victim.

Unfortunately, that raised the question of *who* left the slab... but only Hana knew I was in the dungeon. It was impossible to trace it back to me.

Their conversation continued.

"Most importantly, who left this message behind?"

"They may have a reason to stay hidden, but we can't just drop it.

This is an investigation. Let's ask the trainees and regular adventurers if they saw suspicious individuals inside as they leave."

"Understood."

One of the staff members stepped through the Gate. The other one came to us and lowered his head.

"We're terribly sorry for involving you in this terrible incident. I'm sure it was frightening, but may we ask you some questions to ensure we get to the bottom of this?"

They asked a number of questions. How did such strong monsters appear? What were Yanagi and Katagiri's interactions like? Things in that vein.

Hana faced a volley of questions compared to everyone else. Of course, they didn't believe such a young and inexperienced girl had the power to kill Yanagi. When she explained the story to them, they *seemed* satisfied with her answers. Time would tell.

In the end, the other adventurers exiting the dungeon did nothing to help them reach the truth hidden within me and Hana. We were all allowed to go home.

That night, I told Hana everything: my struggles during the year I was labeled talentless by others, and what came after once Dungeon Teleportation awakened to its true potential. I described how I bypassed the Span to dive as many times as I wanted. I confessed my worries about what kind of dangers I'd attract if others knew I could grow so much faster than them.

Why I felt I had to hide the truth, even from her. I hoped she would understand after what we went through with Yanagi.

She listened quietly until the very end. When I was done, she smiled and nodded with acceptance. I sagged with relief.

There were so many other things I wanted to tell her, but we were exhausted. Better to call it a day.

At least, that was my plan. I had bathed and fallen into bed to recover from both the Remote Magic Tower and the nightmare afterward when a small knock sounded on my door.

"Hana?" I called.

The door cracked open and revealed her clutching her pillow. "Oniichan, can I sleep in your bed tonight?"

I understood. Anyone would find it difficult to fall asleep after a near-death experience. I didn't mind. I moved over so she had room to sleep next to me that night.

How many years had it been since we did this?

"Hey, oniichan?" she whispered.

"Hm? What is it?" I replied.

"Thanks for today. I'm really glad you came to save me."

"...Of course I did. I'm your brother, after all."

I gave her head a gentle pat. She giggled, then went quiet.

"I feel a little sad, though," she said.

"Yeah?"

"I wanted to become an adventurer so I could protect myself without you, but you had to protect me anyway."

"That was your reason?"

I'd wondered why she wanted to become an adventurer.

I never thought she'd tell me at a time like this. Was she was telling me because the incident scared her off adventuring?

"I want to become stronger," she said, contradicting my expectations.

"Stronger?"

"I can't keep relying on you like I did today. In fact, I want to get strong enough to protect other people, not just myself."

"Hmm, gotcha."

Hana was already strong. Maybe not in body yet, but in mind. I was sure she could make her goals into reality. But she was mistaken about one thing.

"I get how you feel, but you don't have to go at this alone," I said with a smile. "You can rely on me anytime. If you stop needing me cold turkey like that, I'll be the one going through withdrawal."

"Jeez. I can't tell if I'm lucky to have a brother who cares this much or not."

Hana covered her head with the blanket. I couldn't tell in the dark, but was she embarrassed? Either way, it was about time we tried to sleep.

"Good night, Hana," I said.

"Yeah. Good night, oniichan."

We slept soundly until morning, just like we were kids again.

EPILOGUE

A FEW DAYS AFTER my duel with Yanagi, I visited the Remote Magic Tower.

"It feels so long since I was last here, somehow," I said softly.

The structure still towered high above me. One week had passed since it first appeared. With some of the novelty worn off, fewer people were there to investigate it. It was a lot easier to avoid the researchers, approach, and attempt to enter the tower.

"Let me try it," I said, placing my hand on the tower. "Dungeon Teleportation."

I waited, but my skill never activated. I wasn't surprised, honestly.

"It really does work differently from other dungeons," I said. I checked my stats display for the description of Dungeon Teleportation.

DUNGEON TELEPORTATION LV 20
REQUIRED MP: 1 MP × Distance (meters)
CONDITIONS: Teleportation can only occur in dungeons that have already been visited.

TELEPORTATION DISTANCE: Maximum 400 meters.

ACTIVATION TIME: 0.8 seconds × distance (meters)

SCOPE: User and user's belongings.

SUB-SKILL: TIME ZERO

Paying 100 MP allows the user to teleport instantly within a
    ten-meter radius. (This ability is obtained when Dungeon
    Teleportation reaches LV 20).

Yup, there it was in writing: maximum distance four hundred
meters. The tower's walls weren't nearly as thick as that, so entering *should* be possible. Why couldn't I?

I had a hunch.

"This dungeon *did* have unnatural elements."

For one thing, each level of the interior looked like a completely different world! Some had *skies* of all things, as if I wasn't
inside a specific structure. Maybe I wasn't inside the tower at all.
What if, unlike other dungeons, it didn't exist where I thought it
did? Its insides could exist somewhere else entirely.

"A dungeon that exists in a space outside of our world,"
I mused. "Is that how the Remote Magic Tower works?"

If my guess was correct, that would explain why the distance
exceeded the maximum requirements for Dungeon Teleportation.
In short, I couldn't grind the Remote Magic Tower like I had
other dungeons.

"I figured this would be the case, but it leaves me in a bind."

I beat the tower, but I didn't receive the third reward. Look,

I wasn't complaining about Battle Barrier, or a strong weapon like Greed, nor the fact it warned me Hana was in danger as a consolation prize, but...I chafed knowing there was more to gain. Call me a completionist, but I wished I could've learned what the prize *was* or the conditions I needed to satisfy to receive it.

Well, there were no time travel skills, as far as I knew. Dwelling on it would get me nowhere.

"Why *did* the system give me information about Hana as a consolation prize?"

At the time, I assumed the information would relate to the mysteries behind the *existence* of dungeons and the level system, not events happening inside one. The system showing me that Hana was in danger suggested it hadn't read my mind so much as read my heart. That shouldn't have been possible for a machine-like system.

Another aspect of the system bothered me. That day Hana was in danger, as I left the tower, right here...

I could've sworn I heard these words:

"You can do it, Rin."

I *knew* the sound of the system, though it was not its usual mechanical voice. The words had emotions behind them, and... somehow, the voice felt familiar.

With my hand on the tower, I asked slowly, "What in the world are you thinking?"

If the owner of that voice was connected with the dungeon and level system in our world, I wanted to know the reason. No, I *had* to know.

Unfortunately, the system didn't respond to me. I sighed in frustration, but I couldn't change its decision. I would turn my attention elsewhere, for now.

"Better head back," I decided. "The more dungeons I dive, the more similar circumstances are bound to turn up. I'll ask the system when the time comes."

I smiled to myself and turned on my heel, leaving the tower behind me. I raised my face toward the sky and strode forward, toward a new future.

That's when fate put her in front of me.

She immediately snatched my attention. Her long silver hair reflected the sun, fluttering in the wind as she walked. She had fairy-tale skin as fair as snow, and eyes as bottomless and blue as the deep sea. Before I realized it, I was standing still. She approached me without hesitation and stopped close enough I could have reached out and touched her. She parted her lips to speak.

"You're Amane Rin, aren't you?" she said. Hearing my name put me at a loss for words, but she continued as if my response wouldn't have changed anything. "I never expected to meet you *here*, but this is quite a fortunate miscalculation."

She regarded me with a soft smile. "My name is Claire," she said. "Amane-san, I came to meet you."

In the distant future, time and time again, I recalled this moment where I met Claire—and how much this instance changed my life.

Thus, the curtain closes on this long prologue. From this moment forward, our story will accelerate to a whole new level.

Rir
An

LEVEL

13617

SP 8710

STATS

HP	106,680
MP	29,490
Attack	25,450
Defense	21,480
Speed	26,620
Intelligence	21,160
Resistance	21,240
Luck	20,220

ACHIEVEMENTS

Dungeon Traveler (10/10)
Nameless Swordsman
Endbringer (ERROR)
Wiser Wise Man

SKILLS

Dungeon Teleportation LV 20
Enhanced Strength LV MAX
Herculean Strength LV MAX
Superhuman Strength LV MAX
High-speed Movement LV MAX
Gale Wind LV MAX
Revitalize LV 1
Purification Magic LV 1
Mana Boost LV MAX
Mana Recovery LV 2
Enemy Detection LV 4
Evasion LV 4
Status Condition Resistance LV 4
Appraisal
Item Box LV 5
Conceal LV 1
Battle Barrier LV 1
Plunderer LV 1

AFTERWORD

ONG TIME NO "SEE," Readers. Yamata here.

Thank you so much for picking up the next installment of my story. This second volume introduces the extra dungeon known as the Remote Magic Tower, as well as new battles and new story elements. Rin continues not only to level up, but he grows in other ways: he gains new skills, weapons, and experience at a terrifying speed. If you enjoyed following him, that would be my greatest joy.

Furthermore, this volume expands on the mysteries and scope of the world of dungeons. I hope you'll look forward to the twists and turns ahead!

This story is being turned into a manga in *Monthly Shounen Ace*. The mangaka, Suzumi Atsushi-sensei, is doing fantastic work. I hope you'll check it out!

Finally, I'd like to thank my editor, S-san, for the continued guidance in this volume; fame-san, who drew such cool and beautiful illustrations; the marketing team; and everyone who worked so hard to bring this story into the world. Lastly, to the readers who cheered me on since the day my novel only existed on the web: thank you, truly, from the bottom of my heart.

I look forward to seeing you again.

—NAGATO YAMATA

FROM THE CREATORS

AUTHOR
NAGATO YAMATA

I live in Osaka and write web novels. For some reason, urban legends have been circulating around Harima these days.

I love tense battles where the main character of a light novel or manga series defeats a strong enemy. I incorporated many of those things into this book. I hope you enjoy it.

ILLUSTRATOR
fame

It's been a while since I drew a school uniform. Gotta love a little sister with a ponytail in uniform!